The Redacted Plays

Orlando Pearson

Paperback ISBN 978-1-78705-672-5
ePub ISBN 978-1-78705-673-2
PDF ISBN 978-1-78705-674-9

Published by MX Publishing
335 Princess Park Manor, Royal Drive,
London, N11 3GX
www.mxpublishing.com

Cover design by Brian Belanger

The Redacted Plays

Foreword

The plays in this collection have as their source my series of short stories, *The Redacted Sherlock Holmes.* These are stories where so extraordinary is the nature of events, they can only be explained by the presence of Sherlock Holmes, although this presence has been redacted from the record.

My works correct this omission so that his influence is made visible for posterity.

A Scandal in Nova Alba, based on Shakespeare's *Macbeth* (Alba is the Gaelic word for Scotland), gives an account of the Scottish king's life far truer to the historic facts than Shakespeare's. The traducing of Macbeth in the Bard's version was driven by James VI's claim to descent from one of Macbeth's political rivals.

As the history books tell us, Macbeth ruled his country successfully for many years, journeyed to Rome to see the Pope, and reclaimed his crown on his return home. All this is reflected in *A Scandal in Nova Alba,* and, in a nod to the Bard, the play has a witches' chorus. We also find out who really killed Macbeth's predecessor, King Duncan.

1

The Baron of Wimbledon is the story of the 1930s German tennis star, Gottfried von Cramm. He was one of the very few prominent Germans of his time who refused to join the National Socialist party, and one of the very few heroes of an unheroic time and place.

This play is a true retelling of the events from his remarkable life which saw him win the French Open tennis championship twice and spend time in a concentration camp. The play makes a jaw-dropping revelation about the relationship between Holmes and Irene Adler.

A Case of Complex Identity is really two plays.

The first half of it is a dramatization of Sir Arthur Conan Doyle's *A Case of Identity*. If the director of a play just wants to perform the Conan Doyle part of the play, the text indicates where that comes to an end. The full version of *A Case of Complex Identity* adds on the sequel to the original story which is *The Camberwell Tyrant*.

The latter shows the truly gruesome end of the villain of Conan Doyle's story, James Windibank, whose departure from this life is swift, exemplary, and drawn straight from ancient Greece. If the director wants to perform *The Camberwell Tyrant* on its own, the start of that play is in the Appendix.

As befits the first ancient Greek tragedy for two and a half thousand years, *A Case of Complex Identity* has a chorus which can be played by a separate group of people or by the main actors.

The Bruce-Partington Diptych is also two plays in one. Both plays can be performed separately.

The first half is a dramatization of Conan Doyle's espionage story, *The Bruce-Partington Plans*. The second half is an account of what happened next to the villain of that story and appeared as a short story in Volume V of *The Redacted Sherlock Holmes* as *The Sleeper's Cache*. This sequel to *The Bruce-Partington Plans* reveals that acting as the British Government, as Mycroft does here, leads to uncomfortable decisions. It is up to the audience to decide whether Mycroft's decisions are justified although it is noteworthy that, whatever one thinks of Mycroft's methods, he achieves his objectives.

This theme is continued in *A Perilous Engagement* where Mycroft again displays his mastery of statecraft in the face of a political scandal which will recall a scandal of very recent times. The choice of name for the female lead, Jean Leckie, is not coincidental and the description of the relationship she has with her fiancé, Ignatius Foley, is an accurate description of the relationship the historic Jean Leckie had with Sir Arthur Conan Doyle.

Finally, *Mr Devine's Original Problem* is a sketch which has Sherlock Holmes being consulted by his most illustrious client about the fate of two expellees from a garden in the Middle East.

Notes on performance

The plays have running times varying from ten minutes (*Mr Devine's Original Problem*) to thirty-five minutes (*A Case of Complex Identity* and *The Bruce- Partington Diptych* in their full-length versions). A running time is also provided before each play which is also preceded by a cast list indicating which parts may be doubled. Female parts are specifically identified. All the other parts can be played by women but in most cases when this is done they should be played as if the actors were men.

Most of the plays can be done with a set of three chairs - one each for Holmes and Watson plus one for the client plus some minor theatrical accessories.

A Scandal in Nova Alba needs a ring, a stage-pistol, and some paper.

The Baron of Wimbledon needs a table, a thermos flask, four cups, and a row of alphabetised lever-arch files. In this play Hermann Göring wields his Reichsmarschall's baton. In performance I have used a wand from a child's conjuring set.

A Case of Complex Identity needs a file containing expense claims, knitting needles, and a door in a frame.

The Bruce-Partington Diptych requires steam-train noises and a newspaper.

A Perilous Engagement needs a fourth chair and a place of concealment for the actress.

There is no need for any set beyond three chairs for *Mr Devine's Original Problem*.

Performance history

A Scandal in Nova Alba was first performed at the Corner House Theatre in Tolworth on 18 April 2018, as part of a run of three performances, again at Sir Arthur Conan Doyle's old house, Undershaw, Hindhead on 12 October 2019, and again on Zoom on 7 November 2020. An audio version appeared in 2019.

The first two scenes of *The Baron of Wimbledon* were premiered in Central London on 27 November 2017. Its full premier is on 27 February 2021. It will be published as an audio-play in the winter of 2020/2021.

A Case of Complex Identity was published as an audio-play in late 2019 and *The Bruce-Partington Diptych* was published as an audio-play in the first half of 2020.

A Perilous Engagement will be published as an audio-play in the winter of 2020/2021.

Mr Devine's Original Problem was premiered as a Zoomcast on 26 September2020. It will be published as an audio-play in the winter of 2020/2021.

All the audio-plays to date were performed by the late, great Steve White. Future audio-plays will be performed by Luke Barton who is already working on audio-versions of my short stories.

A SCANDAL IN NOVA ALBA

Dramatis personae

Sherlock Holmes

Dr John Watson

The King of Nova Alba (can also play Banquo)

Lord Banquo

Fleance (his son)

Running time: 26 minutes

Notes

Any of the roles can be played by women as trouser roles but must be acted as though by men.

Scene I

Theatre is dark

WITCHES:(*Cackling loudly*) DOUBLE, DOUBLE, TOIL AND TROUBLE, FIRE BURN AND CAULDREN BUBBLE. WHEN SHALL WE THREE MEET AGAIN, IN THUNDER, LIGHTNING OR IN RAIN? WHEN THE HURLY BURLEY'S DONE, WHEN THE BATTLE'S LOST AND WON. UPON THE HEATH, THERE TO MEET ...

Suddenly lights go on and we are in the sitting room at Baker Street.

Holmes and Watson are sitting on either side of the fireplace. A door-bell rings off stage.

HOLMES: And here Watson, if I am not very much mistaken, is our next client.

There is a knock on the door.

HOLMES: Come.

Enter King of Nova Alba

KING OF NOVA ALBA: Is one of you gentlemen Mr Sherlock Holmes?

HOLMES: I am. And this is my colleague, Dr Watson. And whom do I have the honour of addressing?

KING OF NOVA ALBA: I am the king of Nova Alba.

HOLMES: Surely, I have seen you before, Your Majesty?

KING OF NOVA ALBA: I think not. This is the first time I have stayed in London, though I did come past your door yesterday to get the perfect spy of the time needed to get here from my hotel.

HOLMES: *(blandly)* Ah, that must be it. And you say you are the king of Nova Alba?

WATSON: *(to the audience):* Nova Alba! That violent fastness in the north Atlantic. The man before us had become king after a power struggle in which his predecessor, King Duncan, had been murdered and everyone apart from the present king and his wife had also been murdered or gone into exile.

KING OF NOVA ALBA: Nova Alba is a country which is much misunderstood.

I have been on the throne ten difficult years, but my realm is now so at peace I was able to go to Rome to meet the Pope. I have never yet been crowned, and I went to see the Pope to ask him to come to perform my coronation for Nova Alba is a Roman Catholic land.

HOLMES: And what was his response?

KING OF NOVA ALBA: He declined my request stating that I was the prime suspect in the killing of King Duncan.

HOLMES: And what was your response to that.

KING OF NOVA ALBA: I asked him how I might clear my name to his satisfaction. He suggested I set up a court of Alban noblemen to try me. If they find me innocent, he will come and crown me king

I would like you to investigate the killing of Duncan and present your findings to the court.

HOLMES: You make yourself very plain.

And … did you kill King Duncan?

KING OF NOVA ALBA: No, sir, I did not.

HOLMES: And did His Holiness not believe your statement to this effect?

KING OF NOVA ALBA: When a man is murdered in his host's house, and, the host acquires the man's titles, lands and fortune, suspicion against the host is a very natural reaction.

HOLMES: And does anyone else know of this plan?

KING OF NOVA ALBA: No, sir. This was something I agreed to with the Pope, who suggested your name himself.

HOLMES: Tell me about Duncan's death.

KING OF NOVA ALBA: I felt my life had reached its zenith when King Duncan came to my castle. He had just made me Thane of Cawdor because of my role in defeating a Norwegian invasion. He came with his two sons, with another nobleman, Banquo, who was had also had a big part in beating the Norwegians, and Banquo's son, Fleance.

After much revelling, we retired to bed at midnight. It was a tempestuous night and I felt restless. I walked around the castle to soothe my nerves. I met Banquo and Fleance. Banquo gave me a diamond ring he said was a gift from the king to my wife:

> "What, sir, not yet at rest?" he said, "The king's a-bed.
>
> He hath been in unusual pleasure, and
>
> Sent forth great largess to your offices.
>
> This diamond he greets your wife withal."

King of Nova Alba draws a brilliant diamond ring out of his pocket.

I curse the day I took this.

My valet found it in my pocket and people thought I had either stolen it from the king after a struggle or robbed it when we discovered his body.

Banquo, Fleance and I talked for a spell and then I went back to bed.

In the morning, we found Duncan's room as a flesher's. The king lay dead in a pool of blood.

HOLMES: So, who was in the castle on the night of the murder?

KING OF NOVA ALBA: The castle had ramparts, an inner courtyard, and a central tower where all the most senior people slept. A porter controlled access to the tower.

Apart from the porter, the only people in the tower were the king, his sons Donalbain and Malcolm, Banquo, Fleance, and my wife and me.

Everyone else slept in rooms built into the ramparts. Outside the ramparts were a moat crossed by a drawbridge and, leading to the drawbridge, an avenue of beech trees.

HOLMES: So, unless an intruder got into the tower and escaped undetected, the killer must be one of these?

KING OF NOVA ALBA: That is so. But ground-level floors were used for storage and had narrow slits as windows so an intruder as killer is unlikely.

Soon after the death of Duncan, the Norwegians invaded again. We beat them back, but not before Dunsinane Castle and its grounds were largely ruined.

HOLMES: So where are these people now?

KING OF NOVA ALBA: My wife is no longer with us. Donalbain and Malcolm fled as soon as their father's body was discovered. They were said to be in England mustering a rebel army but nothing more was heard of them. Banquo and Fleance fled shortly afterwards.

HOLMES: Tell me about these people.

KING OF NOVA ALBA: Donalbain and Malcolm were in their twenties and dutiful sons. Banquo is or was as old as me - a brave warrior and a noble soul. Fleance was fourteen and a bright, charming lad.

HOLMES: Then what is there for me to investigate? You have been on the throne for ten years while your rivals and possible perpetrators of the crime have all fled and your wife has died. Your castle and its environs – which might have given some clues – no longer exist.

KING OF NOVA ALBA: (proudly) For my people I need the affirmation of His Holiness. I will do all a man can do to clear my name. He who dares do more is none.

HOLMES: I will have to think how to proceed. How long are you in London for?

KING OF NOVA ALBA: I am at the Langham Hotel although I may move to other quarters as my sleep is constantly disturbed by demonstrators in Portland Place. If I move, I will send you contact details.

HOLMES: Demonstrators? What are they demonstrating about?

KING OF NOVA ALBA: I had not given the matter any thought but there seems to be one parade after another marching past.

HOLMES: You make yourself very clear.

I require the ring you received from Banquo. It may give me some clues to this case.

KING OF NOVA ALBA: How can this ring still give you clues ten years after the events of which we have spoken?

Long pause during which Holmes is silent but holds his hand out.

King of Nova Alba reluctantly hands ring over, bows and exits.

Holmes sits and thinks before going to a drawer where he pulls out a document.

HOLMES: The King is not the only person interested in who killed his predecessor. I considered taxing him with this document but decided I might find out more if I did not *(Hands document to Watson)*. Do you read out the section marked in red, good Doctor – it uses the same form of English the king used when he quoted his associate, Banquo.

WATSON:*(reading)*

WIFE OF THANE OF CAWDOR

Alack, I am afraid they have awaked,
And 'tis not done. The attempt and not the deed
Confounds us. Hark! I laid their daggers ready;
He could not miss 'em. Had he not resembled
My father as he slept, I had done't.

Enter Thane of Cawdor

My husband!

THANE OF CAWDOR

I have done the deed. Didst thou not hear a noise?

Where did you get this? Whoever wrote it is accusing the present king of Duncan's murder.

HOLMES: I found it in the letterbox marked for my attention yesterday morning. I know nothing more other than that it was delivered by hand, as there was no stamp or postmark on the envelope.

WATSON: So, someone else intimately connected with Nova Alba court has tracked the king to our door?

HOLMES: That is so.

It covers the same events the king of Nova Alba has described to us: his victory over the Norwegians, Duncan's visit to Dunsinane after the battle, the encounter with Banquo and his son after midnight, and the discovery of Duncan's body in the morning.

WATSON: And are there any differences from the king's account?

HOLMES: As you heard, it portrays the king as being goaded into killing Duncan by his now deceased wife. And there are other differences too.

Here, Banquo is killed by agents of the king rather than escaping, and – departing from the implausible to the impossible – it recounts the escape of Fleance, who apparently takes to the skies to flee.

Banquo cries – "Fly, good Fleance, fly!" – his final words before he is slain.

WATSON: Which version of events do you believe?

HOLMES: *(after a pause)* The king is putting his throne at risk by putting himself on trial. He could simply have left the suspicion of guilt to hang over him and carried on.

WATSON: So, what motivates whoever wrote this accusatory drama?

HOLMES: Someone wants to discredit the king and trailed him here.

WATSON: What make you of this second person?

HOLMES: His presence in London must be unknown to the king as he followed the king here to find out whom he wanted to see in London.

You will recall I confirmed the king had been here yesterday morning to check the address.

The second person must be of education to be writing in the extravagant style of the play and must have reason to wish the king ill.

WATSON: And your next move?

HOLMES: I cannot avoid the conclusion that Duncan's killer is in London. We have the king, we have this play, we have unidentified armies of marchers in Portland Place. That covers all the possible suspects. I will continue the investigation in the morning.

Stage goes dark

Scene II

The sitting room at Baker Street at dawn the following morning.

Sound of fighting off-stage.

Sound of the butt of a pistol crashing down on a head and a gasp. Lights come on.

Enter Holmes and Watson dragging a struggling figure at the point of Watson's pistol on stage.

HOLMES: Thank you for rescuing me Watson. I was going out to get newspapers when this beauty pounced. I am not sure I would have won a fight against him on my own.

WATSON: My army service pistol has never been bested

HOLMES: *(to the prisoner)* Who are you?

Silence

Are you Lord Banquo?

BANQUO: How do you know that?

HOLMES: I am Sherlock Holmes. I know what other men do not.

BANQUO: What do you want with me?

HOLMES: I was going to ask you the same question.

BANQUO: I came here to tell you to keep you away from my son.

HOLMES: Fleance?

BANQUO: I am unsurprised you know his name.

HOLMES: Only because I realised you are Banquo.

BANQUO: I followed Fleance here, so I know you know him.

HOLMES: Sir, I have not met your son. I know you have a son, but I do not know where he is or what he looks like. Why do you think I should know him?

BANQUO: My son has a taste for irregular company which I abominate. He has been behaving very strangely over the last few days. I followed him to your door and saw him put something in the letter box. Shortly afterwards, I saw you take my son's letter from the letter box and go back inside. So, I know you know my son.

HOLMES: I received an anonymous document through my door, but I did not know it was from your son of whom, I repeat, I know nothing. I had no idea from whom it was.

Now you tell me what you know about the death of King Duncan of Nova Alba.

BANQUO: *(aghast)* No one has talked to me about that for ten years. What has it to do with you?

HOLMES: Sir, it is normally the prisoner who answers the questions.

BANQUO: Very well. There is not much to tell. I am from Nova Alba. Ten years ago, we defeated the Norwegians in battle. I visited Dunsinane Castle as a guest of the hero of the battle, the Thane of Cawdor. I went with my son, Fleance. King Duncan came with his sons, Malcolm and Donalbain.

We revelled till late and then retired to the central fortified and guarded part of the castle to which only we were permitted access.

During the night, there was a violent storm. I walked round the castle and met my son Fleance who had also been disturbed by the storm. We walked together and crossed the path of Cawdor. And...*(Comes to a halt)*

HOLMES: And?

BANQUO: And the next morning King Duncan was found in his bed dead from a stab wound.

HOLMES: And what did you do?

BANQUO: I did not know what to do.

The likeliest killers were Cawdor and the sons of Duncan. The sons of Duncan fled straight after the crime was discovered.

Fleance and I fled in a hot air balloon shortly afterwards, as I was sure Cawdor, who had seized the throne, was going to have me arrested and put on trial.

HOLMES: And why, sir, do you not mention this? *(Holmes draws the diamond ring from his pocket.)*

BANQUO: *(faintly)* Where did you get that?

HOLMES: No, sir. Where did **you** get that?

BANQUO: I have not seen that ring since the night of Duncan's murder.

HOLMES: And where did you get it then?

BANQUO: I was given it...by King Duncan.

HOLMES: And why did he give you the ring?

BANQUO: *(only just audibly)* He thought I had a taste for glittering baubles. He pressed it on me.

HOLMES: Pressed it on you?

BANQUO: He made it very hard for me to refuse it.

HOLMES: And how did you feel about having it pressed on you?

BANQUO: I felt humiliated, sir.

HOLMES: How 'humiliated'?

BANQUO: My pride was sore wounded.

HOLMES: Anything else?

Banquo runs his tongue nervously over his lips:

BANQUO: As my pride was sore wounded, so I wounded him sore.

HOLMES: You stabbed him?

Banquo nods.

HOLMES: I think I see how the cards are falling. And where is Fleance now?

BANQUO: In our house is a cellar. I locked him in there before I came out.

HOLMES: Sir, you have no right to keep your son in detention. We must to your house presently. I shall call a cab. Watson, do you make sure our friend does not escape.

BANQUO: My house is near Maidenhead, Mr Holmes, and I feel the justice of what you say. I only wanted to stop him mixing in company not meet for a man. In any case, I have just had another son for I have remarried. Though he had a difficult birth with a forceps delivery.

Theatre goes dark

WITCHES: *(cackling)* NONE BORN OF WOMAN SHALL HARM THE KING. THE KING SHALL NEVER VANQUISHED BE UNTIL GREAT BIRNHAM WOOD TO HIGH DUNSINANE HILL SHALL COME

Scene III

A cellar in Maidenhead.

The stage is dark but suddenly lights go on.

Fleance is writing at a desk.

Sound of a key turning in a lock. Holmes, Watson and Banquo enter.

Fleance stands up as they do so.

HOLMES: *(gently)* It is all right. I know everything.

FLEANCE and BANQUO: *(together)* Everything?

HOLMES: I know that you, Fleance, killed Duncan at Dunsinane Castle ten years ago, and I know you did it when the king's friendship towards you changed to lust.

FLEANCE: As my king was fortunate, I rejoiced in heart. As he was my king, I honoured and obeyed him. But as his favour turned to licentiousness, I slew him. I struck out with my ceremonial dagger when he called me to his chamber and advanced on me.

I meant no more than to frustrate him in his pursuit of unusual pleasure, but my blow was a sore dunt which struck home far harder than I intended. He died in an instant.

I left him, joined my father, and gave him the diamond ring the king had given me as a token of his favour. My father passed the ring onto Cawdor when we met him walking round the castle, and said it was a present for his wife.

HOLMES: So why did you put the text of your play through my door?

FLEANCE: My father has always told me I would become king of Nova Alba.

I had heard the present king was in Rome looking to clear his name of the suspicion of having murdered Duncan. I knew he would come through London to get home and guessed he would see an independent investigator.

I followed him off the boat-train to the Langham Hotel and then again when he went out. When I saw him checking out your address, it was an obvious step to implicate him by putting my play about the death of Duncan into your hands.

And my version of events had my father murdered to make sure no false suspicion fell on him.

HOLMES: Why does your father think you will become king of Nova Alba?

FLEANCE: He has always talked about meeting some wild women after the battle with the Norwegians. They foretold Cawdor's ascent to the throne and said my father would be the father of kings.

HOLMES TO BANQUO. I have not had a son, but if I had, I would not be able to blame him for what he did. And I would not rule out taking the blame for a killing he was responsible for. But you should encourage his literary interests, not lock him in the cellar.

BANQUO: I feel the justice of your remarks. *(Embraces his son)* But what is to happen now?

HOLMES: Watson and I must to London to parley with the King.

Theatre goes dark

WATSON: *(to the audience in declamatory style)*: WE SHALL NOT SPEND A LARGE EXPENSE OF TIME BEFORE WE EXPLAIN YOU THE EVENTS JUST SEEN AND SO MAKE US EVEN WITH YOU

Scene IV

A railway carriage.

HOLMES: While political advancement was the obvious motive for the killing of Duncan, it was not the only one.

Apart from the thane and his wife, there were four potential killers – Malcolm, Donalbain, Banquo, and Fleance - but it was Banquo who first crossed our path. The play I received implicated the thane and his wife, and we found out from Banquo that it came from Fleance.

WATSON: But Banquo confessed! Why did you think his confession was false?

HOLMES: A good detective should always test out alternative solutions. When Banquo confessed, I had to ask myself some questions.

Was Duncan more likely to make advances to a burly courtier who could defend himself or to a youth whose silence could more readily be relied upon?

WATSON: Villain!

HOLMES: How likely was a man of Banquo's type to be impressed by a ring with a glistening stone?

And how much more likely was it to impress a callow youth with a head full of poetry?

WATSON: Scoundrel!

I had therefore at least to test whether Banquo's confession was covering for his son. When Banquo said he had locked his son into the cellar, the chance to tax Fleance was too good to miss.

WATSON: And what will you say to the king?

HOLMES: I assume he will want the trial to go ahead although he may not want the full story behind Duncan's death to come out. Once you find one scandal of this type at such a senior level, you are never sure how many more there are. It is hard sometimes even to find an independent judge to investigate.

WATSON: *(to the audience)* The court of Nova Alba noblemen passed a verdict of Not Proven against the king on the charge of murdering Duncan. A Not Guilty verdict was withheld as the actual killer was not identified. This was enough for the Pope to come to Nova Alba and play a small role in the coronation – hence the story of the Vatican cameos.

The king stayed on the throne for another twenty years before abdicating to be replaced by Lulach, Banquo's younger son who, after his difficult birth, had grown to be a strapping lad.

To mark the coronation of Lulach, resident for many years in the area, Maidenhead Borough Council sent a gift of saplings from the famous Burnham Beeches up to Dunsinane to replace the avenue destroyed in the second Norwegian invasion.

So, Burnham Wood really did come to Dunsinane.

FINIS

THE BARON OF WIMBLEDON

Dramatis personae

Sherlock Holmes

Dr John Watson

Gottfried von Cramm – German tennis star

Frau von Cramm (F) – his mother (also plays Irene Adler in the prelude)

Hermann Göring - German Reichsmarschall (also plays Sigismund von Ormstein in the Prelude)

Running time: 21 minutes

Notes

Any of the male roles can be played by women as trouser roles but must be acted as though by men.

Prelude – all voices off-stage

WATSON: To Sherlock Holmes she is always *the* woman. I have seldom heard him mention her under any other name.

Pause

SIGISMUND VON ORMSTEIN: You may address me as the Count von Kramm, although I confess at once that the title by which I have just called myself is not exactly my own.

Pause

HOLMES: I was aware of it. Your Majesty had not spoken before I knew I was addressing Wilhelm Gottsreich Sigismond von Ormstein, Grand Duke of Cassel-Felstein, and hereditary King of Bohemia.

Pause

HOLMES: Miss Adler is the daintiest thing under a bonnet on this planet.

Pause

IRENE ADLER: Good night, Mr Sherlock Holmes.

WATSON: There were several people on the pavement at the time, but the greeting appeared to come from a slim youth in an ulster who had hurried by.

HOLMES: I've heard that voice before.

Scene I

Sitting room of a cottage in Sussex.

Holmes and Watson sitting at either side of a table reading newspapers with cups of tea and a large thermos flask between them. Behind them is a shelf containing some bulky files sorted in alphabetical order.

Dr Watson stands and addresses audience.

WATSON: In 1937, widowed for the second time, I moved down to Sussex to share once more quarters with my friend, Mr Sherlock Holmes. Callers were rare. Our small thatched cottage had a garden with space for Holmes's retirement activity of beekeeping.

On 13 July of that year, there was a knock on the door.

Watson answers.

CRAMM: *(nervously)* I would like to see Mr Sherlock Holmes, please.

Watson brings Cramm into the sitting-room and Holmes rises to greet him.

CRAMM: My full name is Freiherr Gottfried von Cramm. The particle "von" shows that I am of noble origin, but I always call myself Gottfried Cramm. I am an international tennis player.

HOLMES: (*thoughtfully*) Gottfried von Cramm. I confess I am not a follower of sport. Perhaps you could you get down the relevant file from the archives, good Doctor.

Watson makes to get down the K file.

CRAMM: My name starts with a C.

WATSON: I thought that in German the name Kramm normally started with a K.

CRAMM: Normally it does. But not in my case.

WATSON: *(reading)* Here we are. Freiherr Gottfried von Cramm. Amateur tennis player.

HOLMES: Is that all it says? I was expecting some more detail. Your name seems very familiar to me.

CRAMM: I can add further detail if you wish.

HOLMES: Pray do so.

CRAMM: I am the top tennis player in Germany, I have won the French Open twice, and have been the runner-up at Wimbledon three times including in the final two weeks ago. Because of my background I have earned the nickname, the Baron of Wimbledon. Maybe it is under that name that you know me.

It is about my tennis this I would wish to consult with you.

HOLMES: As a consulting detective, sport is not my area of specialism.

Pause

But pray consult.

Long pause

Perhaps it would ease your agitation if you join us for a cup of tea. Two cups for you, I think.

Holmes puts out two cups in front of Cramm, one of which he fills.

CRAMM: Next week I am playing for my country in the Davis Cup against the United States at Wimbledon.

Davis Cup tennis is a team event played over five matches, but the tie is likely to be decided by whoever wins the match between the American, Don Budge, and me.

Budge beat me easily in the recent Wimbledon final. I want your help in turning the tables on him.

HOLMES: My dear Herr Cramm. I am into my eighties, have never played tennis in my life, and you are one of the world's best players. Why do you think I can help you?

CRAMM: You are one of the minds of the age. Of-course you can help me.

HOLMES: And you have come all the way from London to Sussex to ask for my help?

CRAMM: That is so.

HOLMES: And there is nothing else you wish to discuss?

CRAMM: There is nothing else.

HOLMES: This is a busy time of year for beekeeping. I fear I see no point in continuing this interview.

Holmes rises as if to leave. Watson accompanies Cramm to the door.

When he opens it, a mature but dashing and beautiful woman is outside.

CRAMM: Dr Watson, this is my mother.

WATSON: *(to Frau Cramm)* I am afraid my friend cannot provide help to your son on a sporting matter.

FRAU CRAMM: Sporting matter! Did my son not tell you he is being blackmailed?

WATSON: I think you had better come back inside.

Holmes is back at his seat and pours tea from the flask into the fourth cup which he now places at the seat to which he directs Frau von Cramm.

HOLMES: It was obvious, Herr Cramm, that there was no point in you consulting me about tennis. Therefore, there was another matter on your mind. So, I implied that you had been coerced into coming to see me by someone else.

Cramm sips his tea.

And once you had declined to discuss what was really on your mind, it was clear to me that either you would return to London or that that other person would join us.

Accordingly, I set out an extra cup which I left unfilled.

Perhaps you would like to speak freely now that we have been joined by the person for whom that fourth cup was intended.

CRAMM: *(nervously)* In 1932 I made the acquaintance of a famous singer. We were intimate for about three years although I was married for some of that time.

Pause

HOLMES: But my dear Herr Cramm, sportsmen and aristocrats have always had license to indulge themselves in such matters and you are both. What is the shame in this?

Silence

Was there a compromising photograph?

Cramm shakes his head.

A secret marriage?

Cramm shakes his head.

A pregnancy?

Long pause

FRAU CRAMM: (*impatiently*) Mr Holmes, my son is omitting to tell you that his lover was a man.

He is a singer called Manasse Herbst. Herbst was hugely successful on the stage as a singer of operetta. He starred in one show four hundred time. He is Jewish and, when the National Socialists came to power, he was barred from working on the stage and fled Germany.

My son, to my great pride, broke foreign exchange control laws to support him while he is overseas.

CRAMM: I was mad...mad! I had just married and on our honeymoon my new wife became intimate with a French athlete. I did not know what I should do.

FRAU CRAMM: (*pats her son on the hand*) You did what is right. That is what you always do.

HOLMES: What is it you wish me to do?

FRAU CRAMM: One of Herbst's acquaintances was a man called Alfred Wanzer. Wanzer is threatening to tell the authorities about the relationship between Herbst and my son. In Germany, sexual acts between people of the same sex are punishable by imprisonment as they are in Britain. I do not know what punishment my son might receive if the authorities find out what he has done.

We would like your advice on what to do.

HOLMES: (*after a pause*) Has your son given any reason to displease the authorities?

CRAMM: I have refused to join the National Socialist party, although party membership is expected of Germany's elite sportsmen. Hermann Göring, the Reichsmarschall, or marshal of the German empire, is a member of my tennis club, Red-White Berlin. He has tried to persuade me to join, both through blandishments and bluster.

HOLMES: Are you paying the sums demanded by this Wanzer?

CRAMM: I am. You will understand that tennis is an amateur sport and to play it full time, as I do, requires considerable personal wealth which, fortunately, I possess through my family.

HOLMES: Then, I believe your best course of action is to pay the blackmailer, and to be as successful as you can on the tennis court.

FRAU CRAMM: But that is no advice at all other than to continue with the status quo, which is unsupportable.

HOLMES: Consider this, Madame. If your son stops paying his blackmailer, Wanzer will almost certainly denounce him. He may in fact do so anyway.

But if your son plays well on the tennis courts, the German authorities will be much more reluctant to take action against him. They will not want to punish someone who has brought lustre to Germany on the sports field.

The status quo, I regret to say, is the least bad option.

Now if you will excuse me, I must attend to the hives.

Holmes rises. Watson rises.

Gottfried Cramm and Frau Cramm exeunt.

Holmes sits straight down again with Watson.

HOLMES: *(looking puzzled)* Throughout the interview with the Cramms, I felt I was dealing with people known to me, but I could not and cannot remember who that is. The name, Cramm, brings no criminal or client to mind.

WATSON: Well, of course, the King of Bohemia used the name Kramm as his alias when he came to consult with us in the Irene Adler case – *the* woman, you called her - in 1888. The name Kramm then was that of neither a criminal nor a client.

When I first wrote that story I spelt Kramm with a C, but I changed it when I found out that the name is normally spelt with a K in German.

Holmes looks stunned. Stage goes dark..

Scene II

The grandiose office of Hermann Göring in the Air Ministry in Berlin.

WATSON: (*to the audience from the front of the stage*) Within a year Wanzer had talked to the German authorities and Cramm was arrested.

Frau Cramm asked my friend to intercede with the German Reichsmarschall. Hermann Göring on her son's behalf, and Holmes and I travelled to Berlin to meet him.

Göring behind a desk. Holmes and Watson in front. On the desk is a baton.

HOLMES: I have come to ask for leniency in the case of Gottfried von Cramm.

GÖRING: I know your name Mr Holmes from the works of your friend here. And I know Cramm personally. I have tried to persuade him to join our party. I have offered him inducements, and I have made threats. Yet he has refused. He is a very difficult man.

HOLMES: I am not here to discuss Cramm's membership in your party, Herr Reichsmarschall. I am here to appeal for clemency in his impending trial. Cramm is a model sportsman and a credit to his nation.

GÖRING: A credit to his nation! The nation is nothing. It is the race that matters. We Germans regard the acts which Cramm has committed as perverted and repugnant. They will prevent the propagation of our race.

And the English regard such acts the same way.

HOLMES: Whatever he has done, Herr von Cramm has been more than amply punished by his arrest and public humiliation. There is no need to go through with a trial and possible custodial sentence.

GÖRING: On the contrary Herr Holmes, imprisonment of a popular sporting figure like Cramm will show that no one is above the law. We National Socialists want to be seen as harsh but fair.

HOLMES: But the acts took place several years ago in private between consenting adults. Surely bringing them up now serves no purpose.

GÖRING: Bringing them up now has the very desirable effect of focusing the minds of those who might consider opposing us. It will show our opponents that even an aristocrat is not beyond the power of our people's court. My party's full name is National Socialist and that means we represent the interests of German workers. I don't imagine the German workers will care about the fate of an aristocratic tennis player and his male Jewish lover.

Göring rises and picks up an object from his desk which he thrusts into the hands of Holmes

Do you know what this is, Mr Holmes?

HOLMES: It looks like a sceptre.

GÖRING: It is a baton, Mr Holmes. This baton is the baton of the marshal of the Reich. *My* baton. And symbol of *my* power. It is made by the finest German craftsmen as a token of their desire that we perform a sacred duty for our race. And I regard as my sacred duty to see that our form of justice is done.

Göring starts to stride to and fro.

You know, Mr Holmes I am not even sure that we need to go through the nonsense of a trial. In 1934, we had some storm troopers who did some of the things that Cramm got up to. Do you know what we did?

Silence

We had them arrested and executed without trial. And do you know what we did after that?

Silence

We enacted legislation to make what my party had done legal.

My party wants to see that the will of the people for justice is met and to make sure that we live in a country governed by the rule of law.

Our law

Drags Holmes to the front of the stage and points out into the audience

Look out of the window, Mr Holmes. What do you see? Real houses, real people, things that really matter.

What do I care about aristocrats hitting a fluff covered ball across a net?

HOLMES: Is there nothing that can change your mind?

GÖRING: Mr Holmes, if I may say so it is rather amusing to see you trying to play a hand with such poor cards. I am a lover of art, a lover of fine food, and a lover of the chase. Yet you have come all the way to Germany and offered me nothing but bleating.

And now, if you will excuse me, I fear I must bring this interview to an end.

Cramm's trial is next week and I need to think about whom I should appoint as his judge.

Holmes makes to put the baton back on Göring's desk and drops it onto the floor. Göring bellows with anger. Watson picks it up and puts it on the desk.

Stage goes dark.

Scene III

WATSON: *(to the audience from the front of the stage)* To our surprise, Cramm received a sentence of just a year at his trial the following week. This was much the same as he would have got for the same acts in England. He was imprisoned in the Rollwald Concentration Camp and was released after just six months.

In June 1939 he was back in London where Holmes and I watched him win the Queen's tournament, the traditional curtain raiser to Wimbledon.

Holmes, Cramm, his mother and I met for dinner.

A restaurant in London

FRAU CRAMM: How do you find my son?

HOLMES: He looks well, and both his play and his demeanour seem unaffected by his ordeal.

I was surprised his sentence was not harsher and pleased that common sense seems to have resulted in his early release.

Frau Cramm looks straight ahead.

I felt that my interview with your Reichsmarschall had not been a success, though I assume Göring told his chosen judge what sentence to pass.

Frau Cramm looks straight ahead.

I must consider that my involvement in the case was something of a triumph, contrary to what I felt at the time.

FRAU CRAMM: If you felt that your involvement was not a success, maybe it was because evaluating it from feelings rather than from fact-based evidence does not lend itself to a mind like yours.

CRAMM: Soon after you had left Berlin, Herr Holmes, my mother went to see the Reichsmarschall. I think it was the cumulative and persuasive powers of the two of you that had the required effect.

HOLMES: (*surprised*) You did not say, Frau von Cramm, that you had also been to see Göring?

FRAU CRAMM: It was a small matter, and in any case, there is nothing I would not do for my son.

Pause

And when the Reichsmarschall thrust his baton at me, I did not let it fall.

WATSON: Come Holmes. It is time to get our train.

All four rise to part

FRAU CRAMM: *(having shaken Watson's hand, offers Holmes her hand)* Good night, Mr Sherlock Holmes.

At these words Holmes sits back down looking stunned

Exeunt Cramm and Frau Cramm.

HOLMES: (*to Watson*) I have heard that voice saying those precise words before.

Holmes mops his brow. Stage goes dark.

Scene IV

Sitting room of a cottage in Sussex.

RADIO VOICE. This is the news from the BBC in London on Friday 1 September 1939.

Germany has this morning invaded Poland. The British Government is in urgent discussions with the French Government on developments.

On the home front, a black-out has been imposed to avoid giving hostile aircraft any navigational help.

Radio goes silent

Holmes and Watson sitting in a small pool of light.

WATSON: (*to audience*) Since our meeting with the Cramms in June, Holmes had often been absent in mind or in spirit or both.

Once I saw him heading into the railway station just before the London train departed, and once I saw him go into the public library.

But he disclosed nothing to me of what was on his mind although I have never seen my friend so distracted.

HOLMES: I suppose, Watson, that I owe you an explanation of my behaviour over the last few weeks.

WATSON: If I may say so, Holmes, you were often absent in body or in spirit in our years in Baker Street. Your behaviour now reminds me of then.

HOLMES: You will recall the case of Irene Adler.

WATSON: I do. *The* woman you called her. She saw you through your disguise as a clergyman and wished you good night on the steps of Baker Street.

HOLMES: You were not sharing quarters with me at the time of the case in 1888 and so you were not there to observe all that happened next. As you will recall, at the end of the story, Miss Adler married her fiancé, Godfrey Norton, and fled Britain.

WATSON: That was at the end of the story as I wrote it.

HOLMES: She subsequently wrote to me from her honeymoon when her new husband returned to England to seek advice on the medical complaint that subsequently killed him.

I travelled to the south of France where Miss Adler was staying.

Pause. Then Holmes continues in a very quiet voice

I must disclose to you, Watson, that Cramm and his wife are not the only people to have had irregular assignations on their honeymoon.

WATSON: So, you had a dalliance with the adventuress, Irene Adler, on her honeymoon. What has that to do with the Cramms?

HOLMES: Cramm or von Cramm spelt with a C at the beginning is a highly unusual name in Germany. I can find no family records relating to anyone else with a name spelt like that.

I have had a copy of Frau von Cramm's birth certificate sent over to me by what will probably be the last post that will be received in this country from Germany for a very long time. No parent at all is named on it, but the date of birth is nine months after my visit to Miss Adler.

And it was at that time I sent Miss Adler your first draft of the story you call *A Scandal in Bohemia*, which contained the name von Kramm which was spelt with a C in the version of the draft I sent her.

WATSON: And was Miss Adler, *the* woman and apparently your paramour, personally wealthy? Being an amateur tennis player and travelling round the world requires significant personal wealth as Gottfried von Cramm himself stated.

HOLMES: She was an adventuress who mingled with royalty. The swift death of her husband, a wealthy barrister, will have further added to her wealth. There cannot be many single women in Germany who could afford to let their son play tennis full time.

WATSON: So, Frau Cramm is your daughter and her son your grandson?

Pause

HOLMES: I am unable to draw any other inference.

WATSON: And what will you do now?

HOLMES: I not sure that there is much I can do. Even if I wanted to go to Germany and reveal myself to Frau von Cramm as her father and to Gottfried von Cramm as his grandfather, I am not going to be able to do so for the foreseeable future.

I must comfort myself with the memory of the beauty of my daughter, Frau von Cramm, the honourable behaviour of my grandson, Gottfried von Cramm, and the thought that I may survive the gathering storm to see them again when it abates.

FINIS

A CASE OF COMPLEX IDENTITY

Dramatis Personae

Sherlock Holmes

Dr John Watson

James Windibank/Hosmer Angel

Joanna Windibank (his wife) (F)

Mary Sutherland (F)

Mr Westhouse

Mr Connors

Inspector Gregson

Fraser, a constable

Mrs. Castor (F)

Off-stage chorus

Running time: 35 minutes

Notes

Any of the male roles can be played by women as trouser roles but must be acted as though by men.

The chorus can either be played by a separate group or by the players.

James Windibank can double as Inspector Gregson or Mr Connors or both.

Mr Westhouse can double as Inspector Gregson.

Joanna Windibank can double as Mrs. Castor.

Scene I

Stage dark. Voices of Mary Sutherland, Joanna Windibank and Hosmer Angel off-stage.

HOSMER ANGEL: Mary, since we met at the gas-fitters' ball, the bond between us has only grown. And today is our wedding day.

MARY SUTHERLAND: Oh Hosmer, I feel it too. In two hours, we will be man and wife.

HOSMER ANGEL: Now my dear, I have learnt that in life the path is not always straight or easy. Who knows what lies ahead? Will you be always true to me, my Mary?

MARY SUTHERLAND: Always.

HOSMER ANGEL: Will you swear it on this Bible?

MARY SUTHERLAND: (*startled*) You want me to swear to be true to on a Bible? On our wedding day? When I am about to take an oath at the altar? Mother, what do you think?

MRS. JOANNA WINDIBANK: I really think you should do what Mr Angel wants, my dear.

MARY SUTHERLAND: Very well, Hosmer, I swear on this Bible that I will always be true to you.

Scene II

Lights come on to the sitting room at Baker Street

Mary Sutherland is sitting at a table in front of Holmes and Watson. Miss Sutherland's gloves are on her lap.

For several seconds they sit with Miss Sutherland reluctant to speak.

HOLMES: So, Miss Sutherland, do you not find that with your short sight it is a little trying to do so much typewriting.

MARY SUTHERLAND: I did at first. But now I know where the letters are without looking at the key... How do you know my name, Mr Holmes and how could you know all that about me?

HOLMES: My dear Madame, if you would wish to preserve your *inconnu*, it is as well not to let me see the name marked on the inside of your glove when it is placed on your lap. And the hand revealed by the removal of your glove shows the spatulate fingers normal to typists while the bridge of your nose bears the mark of a *pince nez*.

And how may I help you?

MARY SUTHERLAND: I came to you, sir, because I heard of you from Mrs. Etherege, whose husband you found so easy when he was given up for dead.

Oh, Mr Holmes, I wish you would do as much for me. I'm not rich, but I have a hundred a year in my own right, besides what I make from the machine. I would give it all to know what has become of Mr Hosmer Angel. My father, Mr Windibank, takes it all easy. He would not go to the police, so I came to you.

HOLMES: Mr Windibank must be your stepfather, surely, since the name is different.

MARY SUTHERLAND: Yes, my stepfather. I call him father, though it sounds funny, too, for he is only five years and two months older than myself.

HOLMES: And your mother is alive?

MARY SUTHERLAND: Oh, yes, mother is alive and well. I wasn't best pleased when she married again a man nearly fifteen years younger so soon after father's death. Father had a tidy plumbing business, which mother carried on with the foreman; but when Mr Windibank came, he made her sell it. He is a traveller in wines and works for

Westhouse & Marbank, the great claret importers of Fenchurch Street.

HOLMES: Where does your own income come from?

MARY SUTHERLAND: It was left me by my uncle Ned in Auckland. It is in New Zealand stock, paying 4 1/2 per cent. Two thousand five hundred pounds was the amount, but I can only touch the interest.

HOLMES: You interest me extremely. And, since you draw so large a sum as a hundred a year, with what you earn into the bargain, you no doubt travel a little and indulge yourself in every way. I believe a single lady can get on very nicely on an income of sixty.

MARY SUTHERLAND: I could do with much less than that, Mr Holmes, but I don't wish to be a burden while I am at home. Mr Windibank draws my interest every quarter, and I keep what I earn from typing. It brings me tuppence a sheet, and I do fifteen to twenty sheets a day.

HOLMES: I see. And what is the matter on which you wish to see me?

MARY SUTHERLAND: The gas-fitters' gild sent us tickets for their ball as they always did. Mr Windibank did not wish us to go. He never wants to go anywhere. He said the folk at the ball were not fit for us to know, when all father's friends were to be there. At last, when nothing else would do, he went off to France on business, so my mother and I went, and it was there I met Mr Hosmer Angel.

HOLMES: And was Mr Windibank annoyed at your having gone to the ball when he came back from France?

MARY SUTHERLAND: Oh, well, he was very good about it. He laughed, I remember, and said there was no use denying anything to a woman, for she would have her way.

HOLMES: And you say that it was at the ball you met Mr Angel?

MARY SUTHERLAND: Yes, sir. I met him that night, and he called next day to ask if we had got home safe, and after that we met him – that is to say, Mr Holmes, I met him twice for walks, but after that father came back again, and Mr Hosmer Angel could not come to the house any more.

But he used to write every day. I took the letters in in the morning, so there was no need for father to know.

HOLMES: And what did Mr Angel look like?

MARY SUTHERLAND: He was a very shy man, Mr Holmes. He would rather walk with me in the evening than in the daylight, for he said that he hated to be conspicuous. Black hair, a little bald in the centre, black side-whiskers and moustache; tinted glasses. His voice was gentle. He'd had the quinsy and swollen glands when he was young, he told me, and it had left him with a weak throat, and a hesitating, whispering fashion of speech. His eyes were weak, just as mine are, and he wore tinted glasses against the glare.

HOLMES: When did you get engaged to this gentleman?

MARY SUTHERLAND: On our first walk together.

HOLMES: What was his position?

MARY SUTHERLAND: He was a cashier in an office in Leadenhall Street--and—

HOLMES: What office?

MARY SUTHERLAND: That's the worst of it, Mr Holmes, I don't know.

HOLMES: Where did he live, then?

MARY SUTHERLAND: He slept on the premises.

HOLMES: And you don't know his address?

MARY SUTHERLAND: No - except that it was Leadenhall Street.

HOLMES: Where did you address your letters to?

MARY SUTHERLAND: To the Leadenhall Street Post Office, to be left until called for. He said that if they were sent to the office, he would be chaffed by the other clerks about having letters from a lady. I offered to typewrite them, like he did his, but he wouldn't have that, for he said that when I wrote them, they seemed to come from me, but when they were type-written he always felt that the machine had come between us. That will just show you how fond he was of me, Mr Holmes, and the little things that he would think of.

HOLMES: It was certainly most suggestive. It has long been an axiom of mine that the little things are infinitely the most important. What happened next?

MARY SUTHERLAND: When Mr Windibank went to France again Mr Hosmer Angel came to the house again and proposed that we should marry before father came back.

WATSON: Did you not have to seek Mr Windibank's permission?

MARY SUTHERLAND: I wanted to, but my mother said she would square it with him

We were to marry at St. Saviour's, near King's Cross. Hosmer came for us in a hansom but, as there were two of us, he put us both into it and stepped himself into a four-wheeler.

Pause

We got to the church first. When the four-wheeler drove up, we waited for him to step out, but he never did. The cabman said that he could not imagine what had become of him, for he had seen him get in with his own eyes. That was last Friday, Mr Holmes, and I have not seen or heard anything since.

HOLMES: I think you have been shamefully treated. And you think some unforeseen catastrophe has occurred to him?

MARY SUTHERLAND: Yes, sir. I believe that he foresaw some danger, or else he would not have talked so.

HOLMES: But you have no notion as to what it could have been?

MARY SUTHERLAND: None.

HOLMES: How did your mother take the matter?

MARY SUTHERLAND: My mother was angry and said that I was never to speak of it again.

HOLMES: And your father? Did you tell him?

MARY SUTHERLAND: Yes. He thought that something had happened, and that I should hear of Hosmer again. As he said, what interest could anyone have in bringing me to the doors of the church, and then leaving me? And yet, what could have happened? And why could he not write? Oh, it drives me half-mad to think of it, and I can't sleep a wink at night.

Mary Sutherland starts to sob

HOLMES: I shall glance into the case for you, and I have no doubt that we shall reach some definite result. Let the weight of the matter rest upon **me** now, and do not dwell upon it yourself. Let Mr Hosmer Angel vanish from your memory, as he has done from your life.

MARY SUTHERLAND: You don't think I'll see him again?

HOLMES: I fear not. And what is your address?

MARY SUTHERLAND: 31 Lyon Place, Camberwell.

HOLMES: Please leave the letters you had from Mr Windibank here, and remember the advice I have given you. Let the whole incident be a sealed book, and do not let it to affect your life.

MARY SUTHERLAND: You are very kind, Mr Holmes, but I cannot do that. I shall be true to Hosmer. He shall find me ready when he comes back.

Exit Mary Sutherland in tears

HOLMES: The lady's problem is, I fear, rather a trite one.

WATSON: It seems most obscure to me.

HOLMES: I shall discuss the matter with the lady's stepfather. I shall him ask to join us here at six o'clock tomorrow evening. You may wish to be here for then.

WATSON: Are you sure he will come?

HOLMES: I am sure that he too will want this matter resolved.

Scene III

Baker Street.

OFF STAGE CHORUS: WHERE ARE THEY? WHERE IN THE WIDE WORLD TO FIND, THE FAR, FAINT TRACES OF A BYGONE IS BLIND.

Holmes, Watson, and James Windibank.

HOLMES: Good-evening, Mr James Windibank. I think that this typewritten letter agreeing to come here is from you.

WINDIBANK: Yes, sir. I am sorry that Miss Sutherland has troubled you about this little matter, for I think it is far better not to wash linen of this sort in public. Of course, I did not mind you so much, as you are not connected with the police, but it is not pleasant to have a family misfortune like this noised abroad. Besides, it is a useless expense, for how could you possibly find this Hosmer Angel?

HOLMES: On the contrary. I have every reason to believe that I will succeed in discovering Mr Hosmer Angel.

WINDIBANK: *(After a pause)* I am most delighted to hear it.

HOLMES: It is a curious thing, Mr Windibank, that a typewriter has as much individuality as handwriting. Unless they are quite new, no two write exactly alike. Some letters get more worn than others, and some wear only on one side. Now, you remark in this note of yours, Mr Windibank, that in every case there is some little slurring over of the 'e,' and a slight defect in the tail of the 'r.' There are fourteen other characteristics, but those are the more obvious.

WINDIBANK: We do all our correspondence with this machine at the office, and no doubt it is a little worn.

HOLMES: And here Mr Windibank we come to the really interesting matter. I have here four letters which come from Mr Angel. They are all typewritten and not only are the 'e's' slurred and the 'r's' tailless, but you will observe, if you care to use my magnifying lens, that the fourteen other characteristics to which I have alluded are there as well.

WINDIBANK: I cannot waste time over this sort of fantastic talk, Mr Holmes. If you can catch the man, catch him, and let me know when you have done it.

HOLMES: *(Locking the door)* Very well. I let you know, then, that I have caught him!

WINDIBANK: What! Where?

HOLMES: Oh, it won't do--really it won't. There is no possible getting out of it, Mr Windibank. It is quite too transparent, and it was a very bad compliment when you said that it was impossible for me to solve so simple a question. That's right! Sit down and let us talk it over.

WINDIBANK: It—it is not actionable?

HOLMES: I am very much afraid that it is not. But between ourselves, Windibank, it was as cruel and selfish and heartless a trick in a petty way as ever came before me. Let me just run over the course of events.

You married a woman much older than you for her money and enjoyed the use of the money of the daughter as long as she lived with you. The daughter was of a good, amiable disposition, but affectionate and warm-hearted in her ways, so that it was evident that with her fair personal advantages, and her little income, she would not remain single long.

Marriage would mean the loss of a hundred a year. So you conceived an idea more creditable to your head than to your heart. With the connivance of your wife, you covered those keen eyes of yours with tinted glasses, masked the face with a moustache and a pair of bushy whiskers, sank that clear voice into an insinuating whisper, and doubly secure on account of the girl's short sight, presented yourself as Mr Hosmer Angel at a ball she attends.

WINDIBANK: It was only a joke at first. We never thought that she would have been so carried away.

HOLMES: Very likely not. However that may be, the young lady was utterly carried away, and, having quite made up her mind that her stepfather was in France, the suspicion of treachery never for an instant entered her mind.

Windibank groans

But the matter had to be brought to an end in such a dramatic manner that it would leave a permanent impression on her. James Windibank wished Miss Sutherland to be so bound to Hosmer Angel, and so uncertain as to his fate, that for ten years to come, at any rate, she would not listen to another man.

You made her swear on the Bible to be true to you, took her to the church door, and then, vanished away by the old trick of stepping in at one door of a four-wheeler and out the other.

I think that was the chain of events, Mr Windibank.

WINDIBANK: *(Stands up)* It may be so, or it may not, Mr Holmes but if you are so very sharp you ought to be sharp enough to know that it is you who are breaking the law now, and not me. I have done nothing actionable from the first, but as long as you keep that door locked you are detaining me illegally.

HOLMES: (*Unlocking the door*) The law cannot, as you say, touch you. Yet there never was a man who deserved punishment more. If the young lady has a brother or a friend, he ought to lay a whip across your shoulders. By Jove! 'tis well thought. it is not part of my duties to my client, but here's a crop handy. Hold him, Watson!

Holmes and Windibank struggle

WINDIBANK: Let me go! Let me go, I say!

Sound of Windibank fleeing

HOLMES: There's a cold-blooded scoundrel! That fellow will rise from crime to crime until he ends on a gallows.

WATSON: I cannot even now entirely see all the steps of your reasoning.

HOLMES: Well, of course it was obvious from the first that this Hosmer Angel must have some strong object for his curious conduct.

And it was equally clear that the only person who really profited by the incident was Mr Windibank, the stepfather. The fact that the two men were never together was suggestive. My suspicions were all confirmed by his peculiar action in typewriting his letters, which, of course, inferred that his handwriting was so familiar to her that she would recognize even the smallest sample of it. You see these isolated facts, together with many minor ones, all pointed in the same direction.

WATSON: And how did you verify them?

HOLMES: Having once spotted my man, it was easy to get corroboration. I wrote to the man himself at his business address asking him if he would come here. As I expected, his reply was typewritten and revealed the same trivial but characteristic defects.

WATSON: And Miss Sutherland?

HOLMES: If I tell her she will not believe me.

Hafiz has it "There is danger for him who takes the tiger cub, and danger also for who so snatches a delusion from a woman." There is as much sense in Hafiz as in Horace, and as much knowledge of the world.

Part 2

The Camberwell Tyrant

If The Camberwell Tyrant is to be produced on its own, the text below needs to be preceded by the passage in the Appendix.

If A Case of Complex Identity is being produced in full, carry straight on to the next speech.

WATSON: So what will you do now?

HOLMES: I have much bigger fish to fry at present but the biggest fish of all is out of the country at present.

WATSON: I was asking about Miss Sutherland.

HOLMES: I regard that matter as..

Knock on the door

HOLMES: Come in!

WESTHOUSE: I am Lewis Westhouse, the owner of Westhouse and Marbank Wines.

I will come straight to the point, Mr Holmes. We are the largest claret importer in London. One of our buyers, Mr James Windibank, is behaving peculiarly. He is visibly distracted when he is at work, where he spends hours hunched over a typewriter, looking into the distance or distractedly typing.

HOLMES: Anything else?

WESTHOUSE: He has been seen in Camberwell, where he lives, by an employee of the company, escorting a woman who is not only not his wife but also significantly younger than he is. In courting this younger woman, he is reported to have adopted a disguise that could only deceive someone who was either myopic or not overly bright.

HOLMES: And have you not conducted your own investigations into his behaviour?

WESTHOUSE: Our internal investigations have also revealed nothing untoward, and I was minded to close the matter. But then on my way home this evening, I saw Mr Windibank emerge from your front door and flee towards Baker Street Station as fast as I have ever seen a man run.

Pause

If Mr Windibank had been a client of yours, he would not have emerged running from your door. And if he had committed a serious crime, he would not have emerged unescorted. I accordingly believe that you have uncovered something about Mr Windibank and, as the proprietor of W&M, I would like to commission you to investigate Mr Windibank.

Long pause

HOLMES: I have never investigated anyone to see if they have committed a crime without having any idea of what that crime is. This would be an investigation whose consequences are entirely unpredictable and not only for Mr Windibank.

WESTHOUSE: (*After a pause*) I would ask then that you disregard the personalised nature of my questions. Please regard this commission as an investigation into a potential fraud like any other such commercial investigation you might undertake. Our office is in Fenchurch Street, so perhaps it makes sense for you and Dr Watson to start the enquiry there.

HOLMES: Very well, Mr Westhouse. But, more than in any case I have ever investigated, I fear that the outcome may... shall we say... rebound on its commissioner as much as it does on the person being investigated.

OFFSTAGE CHORUS: THE GODS! THE GODS! THEY USE US FOR THEIR SPORT. THEY RAISE US UP, THEY CAST US DOWN, OUR EVERY HOPE THEY THWART.

Scene IV

Holmes, Watson, Westhouse, and Charles Connors – W&M's Financial Controller at the offices of Westhouse & Marbank.

Connors has a large file in under his arm containing expense claims.

WESTHOUSE: Windibank joined us from a firm of importers of Belgian lace about five years ago. He lives in Camberwell as many of our employees do, as our firm used to be based there before we moved to Fenchurch Street. He got married three years ago and invited some of his colleagues to what I understand was a very happy day, though some of my staff commented that his bride, a widow called Mrs. Sutherland, was old enough ... well, at any rate, old enough to know better.

Knock on the door

This is Mr Connors, our Financial Controller. I will leave you with him.

Exit Westhouse

CONNORS: I know your name, Mr Holmes, from the sensational writings of your friend Dr Watson. But what Mr Westhouse is asking you to investigate is a matter calling for financial expertise. This is not one of your typically trivial court cases, and I fail to see how a part-time detective and a retired army doctor can help us when I, as a qualified accountant, have investigated Mr Windibank's affairs and found all is in order.

HOLMES: As you are obviously so well-qualified, it is probably not surprising you are a man with many demands on your time which I am anxious not to waste.

Smile from Connors

And I note that you have an interview for a new position this afternoon, so I would not wish to keep you from that.

Gasp from Connors

Pause

My dear Mr Connors, it is all really rather elementary. Two or even three brand new items of ensemble might be worn on the same day as a matter of chance, but your whole outfit – shoes, suit, shirt, waistcoat, cuff-links, boots – all are brand new, and I note that your hair is freshly cut. Why, you have even gone to the length of removing the moustache that adorned your upper lip in the photograph from W&M's Christmas party which I see behind you. I expect you feel that a moustache does not convey the sobriety that is proper for a man in the position to which you aspire.

CONNORS: I am at your disposal, Mr Holmes.

HOLMES: Let us review Mr Windibank's expenses.

CONNORS: We reimburse our employees for expenses reasonably incurred in the pursuit of company business. Mr Windibank needs to travel to our offices in Bordeaux. He goes there to meet wine growers and traders, to negotiate purchases, and to oversee our bottling plant. When he returns, he claims for his hotel, meals, entertaining and incidentals such as cabs and any other means of travel he adopts to take him to vineyards and wine dealers. Mr Windibank submits his expenses to Mr Westhouse, who authorises them, as he does the expenses of all our buyers.

HOLMES: And how do Mr Windibank's expenses compare to those of his colleagues?

CONNORS: His expenses routinely run at the highest level of our buyers, but, in his position, he needs to travel more often than his colleagues, so that is to be expected.

HOLMES: And where does Mr Windibank stay?

CONNORS: The company has a roster of business hotels in the centre of Bordeaux and has agreed rates with these. Mr Windibank prefers to stay outside the town in one of the beach hotels. He says the air is better there and he can get into the centre of Bordeaux within the hour. Because these are hotels with a predominantly tourist rather than a business clientele, he often changes between them during a trip as these establishments prefer holiday-makers who will stay for a full week or a full two weeks starting on a Saturday. The rate per night Mr Windibank pays is below our roster rate, so this is quite in order.

HOLMES: You make yourself very clear. Could I trouble you to give me Mr Windibank's expense claims for his last six visits to France?

Connors passes over the expense claims and Holmes examines.

HOLMES: Truly a forest of accounting ticks.... but in these April expenses, there is a hotel bill here from 10 March.

CONNORS: It was probably a bill from his previous trip that he failed to submit with his claim for that journey.

HOLMES: But in this claim for March expenses there is another claim for a hotel on 10 March and also one for 26 to 28 February.

CONNORS: How extraordinary!

HOLMES: If I lay all these claims out, I see many nights' accommodation which have been claimed for twice. He had two bills for occupation for some nights in all of his trips and one occasion he had three different bills covering the same night. The bills covering the multiple claims are in each case spread across different expense submissions.

This of course explains Windibank's preference for tourist hotels. He has been making claims against bills he has obtained from other guests. If you ask a fellow guest in a business hotel if you could have his bill, he probably won't give it to you because he needs it to reclaim the cost from his employer. In a tourist hotel the guest is paying for the room himself and so has no further use for the bill. He may even discard it.

Your expense controls are excellent at ensuring the bills were arithmetically accurate, but no one seems to have actually checked the expenses themselves.

CONNORS: I had better call Mr Westhouse.

Exit Connors returning almost immediately with Westhouse

HOLMES: Mr Connors will have explained to you Windibank's fraud. The amount over-claimed amounts to £120.

WESTHOUSE: We should fire him and call the police!

CONNORS: Do you really want this matter to gain wide currency. Our company would look ridiculous in the courts. Far better to ask him to resign and offer him no prosecution on condition he repays the money.

WESTHOUSE: If we go down that route, we may avoid looking foolish, but we will have to provide references for Windibank in the future. That sticks in my craw. I would rather be an honest fool than a clever hypocrite. I will go to his house now and dismiss him myself. And I will tell him to expect a visit from the police. I know how to protect the company's assets from a predator. What is your opinion, Mr Holmes?

HOLMES: Mr Westhouse, this is your decision. You and Mr Connors have set out the main options and you need to make the final decision. Irrespective of what you decide to do, the final outcome is likely to affect you as much as Mr Windibank.

Scene V

Outside a house in Camberwell.

OFFSTAGE CHORUS: OH HORROR! GRIEF! NOT JUST FOR THE LIAR AND THE THIEF! THE VICTIM SUFFERS THE SAME. WHEN THE GODS SO WISH, THERE'S NO LIMIT TO THE SHAME.

There is the sound of furious fighting inside and shouting within including the word "Thieves." Mary Sutherland comes on stage and as she does so there is a sudden silence.

She opens the door, screams at the top of her voice, and then flees off-stage.

Scene VI

Outside the house in Camberwell. Inspector Gregson, Miss Sutherland, Holmes, and Watson plus a Constable.

GREGSON: Miss Sutherland, Mr Holmes and Dr Watson have told me of your personal situation. I would like to hear your statement about last night.

MARY SUTHERLAND: I had been out placing further advertisements for my missing fiancé. When I returned, I heard banging and shouting in the house. When I opened the door, I found an elderly man lying on the floor with his head smashed in and my mother and step-father hanging from the bannister. My step- father had what looked like a flour bag over his head. I fled.

HOLMES: Could you make out what was being shouted?

MARY SUTHERLAND: The only thing I could make out sounded like "Thieves".

GREGSON: Could you formally identify the bodies of your mother and step-father.

MARY SUTHERLAND: *(sobbing)* Do I have to enter that house again?

GREGSON: Is there anybody else, who could identify them?

MARY SUTHERLAND: My mother's mother, Ethel Castor, lives in Bryant Street half a mile away.

WATSON: I will bring Miss Sutherland there and return with Mrs. Castor.

GREGSON: Fraser, would you accompany Dr Watson and Miss Sutherland.

Exeunt Watson, Fraser, and Sutherland

HOLMES: What do you make of the flour sack over Mr Windibank's head?"

GREGSON: That's a new one to me, Mr Holmes. It is hard to see this as anything other than a joint suicide. I've dealt with many suicides by hanging, but none where the victim has covered his head as an executioner covers the head of a condemned man. Could Mr Windibank perhaps have wanted to make his suicide look like an execution after the killing of Westhouse?

HOLMES: And "Thieves"?

GREGSON: That may make sense in the light of the reason that Westhouse came to Camberwell. Let us go inside.

Scene VII

The living room of 39 Lyon Place

The dangling legs of Mr and Mrs. Windibank can be seen in the background.

Westhouse is lying on the floor in a pool of blood.

The blinds are down but the room is lit.

Holmes stoops by Westhouse's body and picks up two knitting needles.

HOLMES: What are these doing here beside the body?

Holmes performs an investigation.

I have examined everything in the house and the only sequence of events which corresponds to the evidence, is that Westhouse forced entry.

There was then a furious altercation in the sitting room, which ended in Westhouse being killed by repeated, savage blows to the head. It must have been Mr Windibank who killed Westhouse, as Mrs. Windibank would not have had the strength to administer such a ferocious beating.

GREGSON: What about the knitting needles?

HOLMES: I can find no place for them. As to the fatal attack on Westhouse – this would be an extraordinary reaction even to being summarily dismissed, as Westhouse said he was going to do to Windibank when we discovered Windibank's fraud last night.

And then for Mr and Mrs. Windibank then both to kill themselves seems inexplicable. Mr Windibank had an acute sense of self-preservation. Even the loss of his position from W&M would have left him and Mrs. Windibank comfortably off. I forecast the day before yesterday that he would end on a gallows. The least likely way I thought it might happen was that it might be one of his own making.

Enter Fraser

FRASER: Mrs. Castor is here.

GREGSON: Don't let her in before we have cover...

Enter Mrs. Castor. Sees Westhouse's uncovered body, screams, and makes to attack it before she is held back by Holmes, Watson and Gregson.

MRS. CASTOR: Oh, the fiend! The fiend!

Struggles violently in the arms of Holmes, Watson, and Gregson before Gregson succeeds in cuffing her and taking her out of the room with Fraser.

Gregson returns

GREGSON: Fraser is guarding Mrs. Castor. Let us draw up the blinds and open the windows. I will cover Westhouse's body.

Does so

Perhaps you Dr Watson could examine the two hanged bodies.

Draws up the blinds

HOLMES: But of course! The blinds!

Gregson, could I question Mrs. Castor?

GREGSON: Of course. I will ask Fraser to bring her in.

Enter Fraser with Mrs. Castor who is struggling in the cuffs

HOLMES: Mrs. Castor. I think I understand the reason for your distress.

Mrs. Castor looks straight ahead.

Did Mr Westhouse seduce your daughter when she was a child?

MRS. CASTOR: *(in tears)* Mr Westhouse used to come to the same church as us. On the annual outing, when Joanna was fourteen, he made her pregnant. We did not think anyone would believe the word of a family of plumbers against that of a wealthy businessman and Mr Westhouse seemed to know what to do to avoid a scandal. He had the child adopted. We never saw it again.

HOLMES: What happened next?

MRS. CASTOR: Soon afterwards he closed down the W&M business in Camberwell and moved away from the area. I have never been able to forgive him for what he did. I kept my counsel when Joanna wanted to marry someone from Mr Westhouse's company, but I never thought I would see Mr Westhouse again. When I did see him, I lost control.

GREGSON: Thank you Mrs. Castor. Fraser will take you home.

Exeunt Castor and Fraser

Although we have established why Mrs. Castor attacked Mr Westhouse's body, it brings us no closer to solving why the Windibanks took their own lives.

HOLMES: My dear Gregson, on the contrary. It tells us everything!

WATSON and GRESGSON *(together)*: Everything?

HOLMES: It explains the deaths of the Windibanks, the flour sack, the reference to 'thieves,' and the knitting needles.

Westhouse knew that Windibank – an amalgam of Westhouse's name and that of his business partner, Marbank – was his son. When Westhouse forced access to the house, he found himself faced not only by his own son but also by the mother of his son, who was married to his son.

Hence the furious confrontation as all three realised what had happened and the killing of Westhouse.

GREGSON: And "thieves"?

HOLMES: The shouting was not about 'thieves' at all but about Oedipus of Thebes. He murdered his father and married his mother. When this was revealed to Oedipus, he blinded himself with pins from his wife's dress. His wife – who was also his mother – hanged herself. I said I did not know where this investigation might lead us, but said Windibank would end on a gallows, which he did. Before he did so, he grabbed the knitting needles with the intention of blinding himself but could not bring himself to do so. The flour sack over his head was the closest he could come to that hideous act.

GREGSON: What shall we do next?

HOLMES: You, Gregson, will have to explain these matters to your superiors, but I see no reason why the details should receive wider publicity. Mrs. Castor does not know that Windibank was Westhouse's child and that her daughter was married her own son. Nor is this something that Miss Sutherland, who is a wholly innocent party in this matter, needs to know. They and the public need only know that Windibank killed Westhouse in a fight which started because the latter tried to fire him from his job. He and Mrs. Windibank then took their own lives after the killing. That explains all the facts and is quite sufficient for public consumption,

Gregson nods and exits

WATSON: Unusually for you Holmes, you look disconcerted by a case you have solved.

HOLMES: My prediction that Windibank would end on a gallows has been precisely fulfilled. And I forecast the final outcome would lead to tragedy for Mr Westhouse. I am troubled indeed that I have acquired the powers of the oracle and grateful that I am now free to focus my attention on the activities of that master- criminal, Pro.....

OFFSTAGE CHORUS: WHAT FATE HAVE THE GODS IN STORE FOR THE MAN WHO SEES TOO MUCH? DOOM AWAITS THEM AND ALL THEY TOUCH. THEY MAY BE CRUSHED IN THEIR OWN FOUR WALLS, OR PLUNGED INTO THE REICHENBACH FALLS.

FINIS

THE BRUCE-PARTINGTON DIPTYCH

Dramatis Personae

Sherlock Holmes

Dr John Watson

Arthur Cadogan West

Violet Westbury (F)

Boy in buttons

Mycroft Holmes

Valentine Walter

Stanley Johnson

Mr Slater

Tyler

Father on train

Boy on train

Running time: 35 minutes

Notes

Arthur Cadogan West can play any other part.

Slater can play any other part other than Holmes and Watson.

Tyler can play any part apart from Holmes, Watson, and Mycroft Holmes.

All the male parts can be played by women.

Part 1

The Bruce-Partington Plans by Arthur Conan Doyle

Scene I

Stage dark at rear but at the front a theatre queue. Cadogan West and Miss Westbury at the back of the queue.

CADOGAN WEST: And we can marry in the new year!

MISS WESTBURY: Oh Arthur, are you sure we can afford to? My mother is a widow. My family won't be able to help us much.

CADOGAN WEST: I have good prospects at the War Office. We will have enough to set up home together and to go to the theatre.

MISS WESTBURY: Oh Arthur!

They embrace.

The footsteps of a passer-by are heard

CADOGAN WEST: Good God!

Cadogan West darts off following the footsteps

MISS WESTBURY: Arthur… Arthur…

After a few seconds wait, Miss Westbury exits in the other direction

<u>Scene II</u>

Light come on to a sitting room at Baker Street. Two chairs either side of the stage with a third chair behind..

Holmes singing tunelessly looking at papers in front of him. Watson standing by the window.

HOLMES: La!…La!…La!…La!

WATSON: Good God, Holmes! Must you sing like that? I can't go out because of the fog, and I can't stay in because of your confounded singing.

HOLMES: I, good Watson, can hear the rest of the choir. Being able to hear the whole work in my head is of the utmost benefit to me for my monograph on that great 16th century Dutch composer, Orlando di Lassus.

Knock on the door

HOLMES: Come!

MISS WESTBURY: My name is Violet Westbury and I have a most peculiar matter to relate.

HOLMES: Pray sit down, Madame.

MISS WESTBURY: I live in Woolwich and my fiancé Arthur works at the War Office premises there. He has been missing since...

An altercation is heard outside the door

VOICE OF BUTTONS: But Mr Holmes is seeing a client.

MYCROFT: Let me pass! Let me pass! I must see my brother immediately!

BUTTONS: Mr Mycroft Holmes!

Enter Mycroft Holmes – bursting in

MYCROFT: Good afternoon, Sherlock. There has been an appalling incident at the War Office premises in Woolwich. We will be joined shortly by...

Sees Miss Westbury

Excuse me for disturbing your consultation, dear Madame, but a grave matter of state has arisen which must take precedence over any private petition.

MISS WESTBURY: Did you say an incident at Woolwich? My fiancé works in the War Office buildings there, and he has been missing since Monday evening.

MYCROFT: Is your fiancé Arthur Cadogan West?

MISS WESTBURY: The same.

Long pause

MYCROFT: Madame, I am sorry to tell you that your fiancé has been found dead, and it is about his death that I have come to see my brother.

Violet Westbury screams.

MISS WESTBURY: I feared as much. Was it an accident?

MYCROFT: Madame, I very much fear it was not, and the circumstances of your fiancé's death seem, I regret to say, most discreditable to him.

HOLMES: Mycroft, my client has had a grave shock and may be able to assist us with any enquiries we wish to make. Watson, if you could bring Miss Westbury a glass of water, she could perhaps give us a fuller account of the disappearance of her fiancé. I fear that what Mycroft has to say will involve matters of state, Madame, and you will not be allowed to be privy to that, but the good Watson will accompany you home.

Watson brings a glass of water and Miss Westbury sips at it

MISS WESTBURY: What I have to say is brief. My fiancé and I were in the queue waiting to get into the Woolwich Theatre. The fog was so thick that the gas lamps failed at twenty feet. Suddenly, he uttered an exclamation and vanished into the fog.

HOLMES: And did you see or hear anything before he disappeared?

MISS WESTBURY: I heard the footsteps of someone walking past but I could see nothing in the fog. After waiting for a few minutes, I went home.

HOLMES: And had your fiancé showed any signs of strain in recent weeks?

Pause

Come now Miss Westbury. I must ask you to be frank even if it seems to tell against your fiancé.

MISS WESTBURY: Indeed, there is not much to tell.

He spoke one evening of the importance of the secret although I knew better than to ask what the secret was. I have some recollection that he said that no doubt foreign spies would pay a great deal to have it.

But that was all.

But you have not told me about how my fiancé met his end.

MYCROFT: I fear that as, as my brother has indicated, I am somewhat restricted in what I can tell you about your fiancé.

MISS WESTBURY: Please tell me what you can. I am not easily shocked.

MYCROFT: Papers relating to the biggest secret your fiancé was involved in are missing. His body was found yesterday morning beside the rail-track at Aldgate station. He had suffered a severe head wound consistent with a fall from a train. In his wallet were tickets to the theatre and some loose change. We assume he was assaulted on the train and that his attacker through threw the body from the carriage.

I can tell you no more Madame, but I must now consult with your brother.

HOLMES: Watson, could you accompany Miss Westbury back to Woolwich. I will meet you at Aldgate station at twelve.

MISS WESTBURY: Oh, Mr Holmes! If only you could save Arthur's name. His job meant everything to him. He would have cut off his right hand rather than betray a government secret.

Exeunt Watson and Westbury. Sound of door closing.

HOLMES: So, Mycroft. What was this secret?

MYCROFT: The documents found in Cadogan West's pocket relate to the Bruce- Partington submarine. Miss Westbury is right to say that a foreign power would pay a lot for these as I can assure you that naval warfare for any enemy craft becomes impossible within the radius of a Bruce-Partington's operation.

HOLMES: So, anyone with the missing papers could build the submarine?

MYCROFT: Cadogan West was a clerk at Woolwich and his superior was a Mr Stanley Johnson who can give you the technical details on the plan. I have asked him to join us, and he is waiting in the corridor downstairs for me to say to him that he can join us. The man in charge of the security papers was Sir James Walter. I saw him yesterday, but I sent a message to him to come join us here so that you could talk to him.

Knocking on the door

That may be he. Come in!

VALENTINE WALTER: Is one of you gentlemen Mr Mycroft Holmes?

MYCROFT: I am, and this is my brother Sherlock Holmes. Who are you?

VALENTINE WALTER: I am Colonel Valentine Walter, the brother of Sir James Walter. Sir James died this morning and, given the serious matters that have arisen, I thought I should come here and tell you this as I saw you had asked him to join you here.

MYCROFT and HOLMES TOGETHER: Sir James Walter is dead!

VALENTINE WALTER: He was found dead in his bed. A doctor is investigating the cause. I was called to the house and have only come away when I was passed the note asking that he come here.

HOLMES: And you can throw no light on the matter?

VALENTINE WALTER: My brother and I were close, so he spoke to me briefly on the matter of the missing papers yesterday. He said he had no doubt that a junior clerk called Cadogan West was guilty. But I know nothing more myself and you will both understand that I have much to attend to and must return to my brother's distraught family.

Exit Valentine Walter

HOLMES: I will need from you, Mycroft, a list of all the known spies in London. Such a matter would not have been dealt with by a small player.

MYCROFT: I have it here.

Gives Holmes a piece of paper

HOLMES: You anticipate my every need, brother.

MYCROFT: The only men worth considering are Adolph Mayer, of 13 Great George Street, Westminster: Louis La Rothière, of Campden Mansions, Notting Hill: and Hugo Oberstein, 13 Caulfield Gardens, Kensington.

I will now ask Mr Stanley Johnson to join us.

Mycroft goes to the door

Mr Johnson will you come up, please?

Enter Stanley Johnson

HOLMES: Good morning Mr Johnson. Perhaps you could you tell us something about yourself.

JOHNSON: I have worked at the war-office in Woolwich for twenty years and am the senior draftsman of technical plans. I am always the last man out of the office, and on Monday I locked up as usual with the papers in the safe.

HOLMES: And you cannot account for their absence?

JOHNSON: I cannot – beyond to say that the papers are still missing, that Cadogan West was missing, and that his body has now been found.

I beg you won't try to drag me into the matter, Mr Holmes. What is the use of our speculating when the evidence is so unequivocal?

HOLMES: And anyone with these papers could construct a Bruce-Partington submarine?

JOHNSON: So I have reported to the Admiralty although there is a new paper on self-adjusting slots which is being prepared by an engineer in Portsmouth. But whoever has the papers would be able to find a way round the absence of one detail.

HOLMES: Thank you Mr Johnson. You have been very clear.

MYCROFT: You may return to Woolwich, Mr Johnson.

Exit Johnson

HOLMES: Was a ticket found on Cadogan West's body? That would show the station nearest to his killer's house.

MYCROFT: No ticket was found. The police assume the assailant took it to prevent us discovering precisely that.

HOLMES: It looks bad for Cadogan West. He had the motive with the need for money for his wedding and he had the opportunity. But if he is the criminal, our trail is at an end as the plans will be being sold abroad to the highest bidder on the Continent as we speak. What is there that remains to do?

MYCROFT: To act, Sherlock, to act. All my instincts are against this being the end of the trail.

HOLMES: I'll to Aldgate now to meet Watson. I will ask to be shown where the body was found. I fear all the queen's horses and all the queen's men will not avail us here.

Scene III

Aldgate station

Steam trains can be heard in the background

Holmes and Watson

WATSON: So, what is there to do here?

HOLMES: This is where the body was found. We will be joined shortly by Mr Slater who found it and we will see what clues the scene affords us of this dark matter.

WATSON: And what has your brother Mycroft to do with this? You told me he had a position under the British Government.

HOLMES: I did not know you quite so well then. One must be discreet when one talks of high matters of state. You are right in thinking that he is under the British government. You would also be right in a sense if you said that occasionally he IS the British government.

WATSON: My dear Holmes!

HOLMES: I thought I might surprise you. My brother has the tidiest and most orderly brain, with the greatest capacity for storing facts, of any man living. The conclusions of every department are passed to him. All other men are specialists, but his specialism is omniscience.

If a minister needs information as to a point which involves the Navy, India, Canada, and the bimetallic question, he could get his separate advices from various departments on each. But Mycroft can focus them all and say offhand how each factor would affect the other. Again and again his word has decided the national policy.

But here comes Mr Slater. We must defer further discussions for another time.

Enter Slater

SLATER: Good afternoon, good sirs. I am a track-bed layer, and I was here at 6 on Tuesday morning to go down the tunnel to put some more ballast into the track. I found the body right here, sir, just at the mouth of the tunnel where the train emerges as it comes into the station.

HOLMES: And yet there seems to be no sign of bleeding here.

SLATER: There was very little, sir, either on the ground or on the body although the wound had crushed in the skull.

HOLMES: Does that strike you as likely Watson?

WATSON: Wounds may be fatal but sometimes they do not bleed much if the bone is broken but not the skin.

Pause

HOLMES: *(Surveys the scene)* I suppose there are very few sets of points on the Underground.

SLATER: No indeed sir. This is one of the few places. This is where the Metropolitan line and the Circle line join to run on the same track.

HOLMES: By Jove! Points and a curve! If only it were so. I have been dim indeed not to see the possibilities.

Long silence

SLATER: I'll be about my business, sir.

Exit Slater

HOLMES: It's like this Watson. We could not account for a lack of a ticket on Cadogan West's body and he bled very little at his final resting place. And yet his body is found on one of the very few places on the Underground where there are points and a curve.

WATSON: What of it?

HOLMES: I believe that Cadogan West met his end elsewhere and that he was placed on the roof of the train. Points and a curve would affect nothing within the train. That would explain the lack of bleeding and the lack of a ticket.

WATSON: What difference does that make?

HOLMES: I noticed that one of the spies on the list that Mycroft gave me, had a house that backed onto the Underground.

Let us to the house of Oberstein at Caulfield Gardens and see what there is to see.

Scene IV

WATSON: *(to audience)* I had no idea that, when my friend said that we were going to look at Oberstein's house in Caulfield Gardens, he meant...

Sound of exertion as a window is forced open

HOLMES: I've forced the lock back, Watson. We can go through here.

WATSON: You might get us arrested, Holmes.

HOLMES: In prison for Queen and country, eh, Watson? I know I would do that, and I fancy you would too.

At another window.

Look over here Watson. A blood stain on this ledge.

WATSON: But how could a body be placed on a moving train?

Sound of a train approaching and then coming to a halt with screeching brakes.

Pause

Sound of a train moving off.

HOLMES: Cadogan West met his end here and the murderer disposed of his body by placing it on the roof of the train. The trains are held by a signal here before entering Kensington Station. That was why his body was found where it might be expected to fall off the roof of a train carriage – at a set of points on a curve.

WATSON: You have never risen to greater heights.

HOLMES: I cannot agree. The matters I have elucidated to you were obvious once I had noted where the body fell and the location of Oberstein's house overlooking a place where the Underground stops.

I will now go through the house. Listen carefully for anyone approaching although there is every sign – curtains drawn, shutters closed, larder empty - that Oberstein has left. I see he reads the *Daily Telegraph* and you might like to look through some old editions to pass the time.

Watson seats himself with a newspaper while Holmes carries on searching

WATSON: Holmes! Oberstein has circled an entry in the agony column of the paper

Listen to this

"Matter presses. Must withdraw offer unless contract completed.

Pierrot".

Picks out another newspaper

And this

"Monday night after nine. Two taps. Only ourselves. Do not be so suspicious. Payment in hard cash when goods delivered.

Pierrot"

HOLMES: By Jove, we've got him, Watson.

WATSON: Got him?

HOLMES: There is at least an even chance we will reel in our man. We will be back here the day after tomorrow with Mycroft.

Scene V

Oberstein's House

Holmes, Mycroft and Watson

HOLMES: We may have some time to wait so I can elucidate to you my thought processes in solving this case.

We could not account for why Cadogan West should have bought tickets for the theatre with his fiancé and then suddenly left her in the fog.

It may have been a blind but a very singular one.

We are here because I assume there was another person whom Cadogan West had reason to suspect and whom he saw in the fog in Woolwich. He followed this other person from Woolwich to here where he met a violent end.

MYCROFT: What can you tell us about the other person?

HOLMES: Nothing except that he corresponded with Oberstein through the agony column of the Daily Telegraph.

MYCROFT: But what are we doing here? Oberstein has left London and this other person is hardly likely to return.

HOLMES: Pierrot has placed another advertisement in today's Telegraph.

MYCROFT: What!

Here it is:

"Tonight. Same hour. Same place. Two taps. Most vitally important. Your own safety at stake.

Pierrot"

MYCROFT: By George! If he answers that we've got him!

HOLMES: That is what I thought when I placed the advert.

I would point out that my chain of reasoning is based on the theory that there is another person in this case. If, in spite of all the evidence to the contrary, Cadogan West was the person who abstracted the plans, then we are wasting our time. The malefactor is dead, and the papers are unrecoverable. There is an even chance that the true felon will read my advertisement and come here.

Silence and darkness

Footsteps heard outside

HOLMES: It is he. Leave this to me.

Furtive knock

Holmes opens the door and propels the person outside into the room

Lights come on and it is Valentine Walter.

HOLMES: Well you can write me off as an ass this time, Watson. This is not the bird I was looking for.

VALENTINE WALTER: What is this? I came to see Herr Oberstein?

HOLMES: Everything is known, Colonel Walter. How an English gentleman could behave in such a manner is beyond my comprehension. You transacted a squalid bargain with a spy. You abstracted the secret papers for him, and you were seen and followed by young Cadogan West, who had probably some previous reason to suspect you. Leaving his private concerns, like the good citizen he was, he followed you closely in the fog and kept at your heels until you reached this very house. There he intervened, and then it was, Colonel Walter, that to treason you added the more terrible crime of murder.

VALENTINE WALTER: I did not! I did not! Before God I swear that I did not.

HOLMES: Tell us, then, how Cadogan West met his end before you laid him upon the roof of a railway carriage.

VALENTINE WALTER: I will. I swear to you that I will. I did the rest. A Stock Exchange debt had to be paid. I needed the money badly. Oberstein offered me five thousand. It was to save myself from ruin.

HOLMES: Tell us then what happened.

VALENTINE WALTER: Cadogan West had his suspicions before. I never knew he was behind me until I was at the very door. I had given two taps and Oberstein opened. The young man rushed up and demanded to know what we were about to do with the papers. Oberstein had a short life-preserver and struck Cadogan West on the head. The blow was a fatal one. He was dead within five minutes. It was Oberstein who had the idea of putting Cadogan West on the roof of a train and that was the end of the matter so far as I was concerned.

HOLMES: Can you not make reparation? It would ease your conscience, and possibly your punishment.

VALENTINE WALTER: What reparation can I make?

HOLMES: Where is Oberstein with the papers?

VALENTINE WALTER: I do not know.

HOLMES: Did he give you no address?"

VALENTINE WALTER: He said that letters to the Hotel du Louvre, Paris, would eventually reach him.

HOLMES: Then reparation is still within your power.

Here are paper and pen. Sit at this desk and write to my dictation.

"Dear Sir

"With regard to our transaction, you will no doubt have observed by now that one essential detail is missing. I have a tracing which will make it complete. This has involved me in extra trouble, however, and I must ask you for a further advance of five hundred pounds. I shall expect to meet you in the smoking-room of the Charing Cross Hotel at noon on Saturday."

That will do very well. I shall be very much surprised if it does not fetch our man."

WATSON: (to audience) And so it did! Oberstein, eager to complete the coup of his lifetime, came to the lure and was arrested. The plans were found in his trunk As to Holmes, he returned refreshed to his monograph upon the Polyphonic Motets of Orlando di Lassus.

Part 2

The Sleeper's Cache

Scene VI

Baker Street

WATSON: *(to audience)* After the capture of the spy Oberstein and the recovery of the Bruce-Partington submarine plans, Holmes dedicated his attention to his work on 16th century music.

What follows now started on 27 December 1895.

HOLMES: *Sings tunelessly but loudly*

La! *Pause*

La! *Pause*

La!

WATSON: Must you sing like that?

HOLMES: Not for much longer. I have nearly finished my monograph on the polyphonic motets of Orlando di Lassus. Another week unless another case intervenes.

Knock on the door

Come in!

Enter Violet Westbury

HOLMES: Good evening Miss Westbury.

MISS WESTBURY: Good evening Mr Holmes. I have come to you straight from the Old Baily where I went to hear the sentencing of Hugo Oberstein and Valentine Walter, the murderers of my fiancé.

HOLMES: And what sentence was passed?

MISS WESTBURY: (*outraged*) Valentine Walter, who stole the submarine papers and was present when the blow was struck, did not face a murder charge. He got two years. Oberstein, who struck the blow that killed dear Arthur, got fifteen. And I am sure he will be out in less. I and my widowed fiancé's mother now face a life sentence.

I was at her house two days ago for Christmas, and we spent the day in tears. I do not believe that she is long for this world.

HOLMES: I understand your concern, Madame. Your fiancé's conduct exemplified everything that is right about our public servants – he saw his country in peril, he risked his life to defend it, and he paid the ultimate price. Murder and treason are crimes which normally require a capital punishment for their expiation. These sentences make the crimes cheap.

You and your fiancé's mother are the most direct victims, but the whole country is the poorer for the death of your fiancé.

Enter Mycroft Holmes

MYCROFT: I should have knocked, Sherlock, but my matter is exceedingly urgent. (*Sees Miss Westbury*) Good evening Miss Westbury. I have a most pressing matter of state to discuss with my brother. I must ask you to leave us.

HOLMES: Miss Westbury, I am fully apprised of your concern. I will ensure that you receive a response.

Exit Westbury. Sound of door closing.

To Mycroft

Miss Westbury was expressing her concern at the low sentence Oberstein received for the murder of her fiancé. It is not my custom to intervene on sentencing but……

MYCROFT: (*distractedly*) Well, obviously, we agreed to a low sentence with the Germans in exchange for their understanding on another matter. That's why we arranged sentencing for between Christmas and the New Year. No one reads the papers much at this time of year, and people will have forgotten about it before they go back to work next week.

It is in regard to Oberstein that I would wish to consult with you now.

HOLMES: You have made a squalid bargain with the Germans for Oberstein who had murdered a British public servant who was defending this country's interests? I am sure that if Cadogan West had stolen the papers that Oberstein committed murder for, he would have got a much higher sentence than Oberstein has now got.

MYCROFT: Sherlock, your skills lie, if I may so, in the forensics of investigation and not in matters of statecraft. It is most unwise of you to regard the bargain we have made with the Germans as squalid.

And you are of course right to say that Cadogan West would have been given a much longer sentence for stealing the submarine papers than Oberstein has got now. Public servants need to be aware that they must not leak state secrets, or the business of government becomes impossible

I shall now elaborate on the matter arising from the Oberstein affair that I wish to consult you on now.

Pause

HOLMES: *(uncertainly)* Pray continue.

MYCROFT: Events have proceeded at a much more precipitate speed than we anticipated. In order to seal our deal with the Germans, we have agreed to hand Oberstein over to the Germans now for what will probably be just a short period in their custody. I fear I cannot disclose, even to you, the matter over which this deal has been struck.

HOLMES: I see.

MYCROFT: Spies normally conceal documents on sensitive matters to make themselves more valuable in the event of arrest – lists of people over whom they have a hold, codes to safes, and so on. To secure whatever documents Oberstein may have concealed, Mr Tyler, one of our espionage people, has been acting as Oberstein's cellmate in Wandsworth Prison.

HOLMES: And what has he found out?

MYCROFT: Mr Tyler is waiting downstairs, and I will now ask him to join us.

Goes to the door.

Mr Tyler, you can come up.

Enter Tyler

TYLER: I have been Oberstein's cellmate since he was taken into custody. I introduced myself to him as a prisoner on a charge of tax evasion, and he told me that the charge against him was the forging of bearer bonds. He was very reluctant to establish any sort of relationship with me, but the long hours of being locked in a cell gradually meant that he started to speak more freely.

HOLMES: And did he disclose anything of interest?

TYLER: He has been endlessly evasive. 'I kept it all under the bed,' he said at one point.

MYCROFT: We had of course searched under the floors of Oberstein's residence in Caulfield Gardens, as well as looking in all the obvious places such as under his bed.

TYLER: At another point he said that he kept all his best secrets in the mouth.

MYCROFT: He had a cyanide capsule in a gum cavity when he was arrested but we were able to prevent him from ingesting its contents.

TYLER: On another occasion, he said he had hidden his secrets where the sun doesn't shine.

MYCROFT: Oberstein had spent time spent in Australia and in the United States and that may be where he might have learnt such a vulgar expression.

HOLMES: This all sounds like a show of defiance rather than the transmission of information. Did he say anything else?

TYLER: Oberstein has a restless sleeping pattern. He snores and is given to talking in his sleep. Last night he repeated the expression that his secrets were hidden where the sun didn't shine, but added, 'or only once a year.'

HOLMES: That seems rather more specific. So, I take it, Mycroft, you want me to identify where any documents or other material might be from these clues?

MYCROFT: That is so. And it must be by midnight tomorrow night as that is when we are handing him over to the Germans.

HOLMES: *(To Tyler)* Und wo haben Sie Ihr Deutsch gelernt?

Tyler looks at Mycroft with a puzzled expression.

MYCROFT: Tyler had no need to know any German, Sherlock. The ability to do so would have aroused suspicion in Oberstein. And in any case, Oberstein spoke perfect English.

HOLMES: I see.

Long silence

MYCROFT: Are you going to take on this case?

Long silence

But Sherlock, the security of our country depends on us finding whatever Oberstein has concealed. Once he has been handed over, the data will either be lost altogether or fall into the hands of this country's enemies. Your patriotism will tell you that you must accept this commission.

HOLMES: I will need some time to think, Mycroft. Your proposal has thrown up several major dilemmas.

Exeunt Mycroft and Tyler

WATSON: Surely someone in Mycroft's position knows what lies in this country's interests, and we must take him at his word?

HOLMES: I confess, Watson, the clues with which Tyler has furnished us are so *outré* as to make this commission hard to resist. I must say, however that, I am reluctant to do so when I find the objective of my investigation is to enable Oberstein to evade British justice.

Let us check the train times to Salisbury. We are going to Stonehenge or the hanging stones.

WATSON: The hanging stones?

HOLMES: That is the meaning of the word henge, but I use the term only because it is on a gallows that I think Oberstein should be.

WATSON: And why Stonehenge?

HOLMES: I shall explain that on the train from Waterloo tomorrow.

I will send a message to Mycroft to say we will take the case.

Scene VII

WATSON: *(to the audience)*

Train noise in the background.

We were lucky to be able to head for Stonehenge the next day. Waterloo Station was closed for engineering works, and it took a dash in a hansom to get us to Paddington for the Great Western Railway train heading to Bath.

A train to Bath

Father, boy, Holmes, and Watson

HOLMES: The art of the logician is to separate the specific from the general, good Watson. The references to a mouth and a bed are vague in the extreme and may even not be relevant to our search. But Stonehenge is famous for being so constructed that the sun shines through carefully positioned gaps between the stones at dawn on the winter and summer solstices. That is where we must seek the cache concealed by the restlessly sleeping Oberstein.

I would beg of you not to talk to me for the present as I must give this case some thought.

FATHER: *(to his son):* The Romans built the baths at Bath or Aquae Sulis as they called it. You can tell your Latin teacher about it when you go back to school. Bath is the only place in Bri..

BOY: Did you know, father, that Brunel originally built this line with a seven-foot gauge rather than the four foot eight-and-a half inch gauge in use almost everywhere else?

FATHER: Why did he do that?

BOY: It ensures smoother running of the train.

FATHER: So why don't other lines run on a seven-foot gauge?

BOY: The extra width made building bridges and tunnels more expensive. After Chippenham, we go through the Box Tunnel which is two miles long - the longest tunnel in the world. You can imagine how having tracks over two fifths wider than normal made building a tunnel more expensive.

The navvies who built the tunnel did so by digging tunnels from opposite sides of the hill and did their digging so precisely that when they met the two tunnels were only two inches misaligned. Brunel was so pleased at the work that he gave the foreman his signet ring.

Looking out of the window.

We are going at over sixty miles an hour into the tunnel

Stage goes dark.

HOLMES: But of course!!

Deafening screech of brakes

Lights come on after a few seconds

Holmes and Watson at the western mouth of the Box Tunnel

WATSON: What are we doing here? This isn't Stonehenge.

HOLMES: *Shines a lantern into the air*

This is the place where we must seek the sleeper's cache. When Brunel built the Box Tunnel, he had it cut so that the sun shines right through it at dawn on his birthday on the ninth of April and on that date only.

Let us see what we can find here in the brick facings of the tunnel mouth where the sun shines only once a year. The soot from the trains should show where anything has been recently disturbed.

WATSON: But Holmes! You are forgetting the clue about the cache being under Oberstein's bed. You should look in the clinker of the track-bed under the sleepers.

HOLMES: *(Click of impatience from Holmes)* Look at this Watson! A tin box here in the ballast!

Pulls out a box and opens it

Very strange. The names and addresses are all in the United States.

Never mind. This is clearly what we are looking for.

Let us stop the next train to London and then we will bring Oberstein's cache to Mycroft. We should just be in time.

Scene VIII

WATSON: *(to audience)* We got back to Paddington at 11.15 and a dash in a hansom across London got us Mycroft's ministry.

MYCROFT: *(Very distracted)* What is it?

HOLMES: I am happy to say, brother Mycroft, that I have been successful in finding Oberstein's documents.

MYCROFT: So that's what you have been doing all day?

HOLMES: Yes, that was your request to me from yesterday. You wanted this document here by midnight and we have just made it.

Long pause

The names on the documents seem to be in the United States.

MYCROFT: Yes, that makes sense.

Long pause

As I told you, Oberstein's posting before London was Washington. But I would beg you, Sherlock, and you too, Dr Watson, to leave me in peace. For goodness sake, Sherlock, and you too Dr Watson, please leave now.

In rising panic

Get out of my office at once!

Scene IX

WATSON: *(to audience)*

We returned to Baker Street, and life continued much as before Mycroft's visit.

Holmes singing tunelessly again with papers in front of him while Watson reads a newspaper.

HOLMES: La!..La!..La!..La!

WATSON: Have you not finished your monograph?

HOLMES: I am not progressing much at the moment as I remain curious about Mycroft's behaviour.

He could not have behaved in a way more likely to attract suspicion, but I do not know what cause he would have to be scared of me.

Has the hand-over of Oberstein been announced?

WATSON: No, I am as puzzled about it as you.

I assume it was about what the newspapers are calling the Jamieson Raid in the Transvaal.

The return of Oberstein was obviously in exchange for the German forces in South West Africa staying out of it. But no announcement of Oberstein's release has been made.

HOLMES: There are three alternatives as to what has happened.

Oberstein has been handed over, but no announcement of his release into German custody has been made. This strikes me as unlikely, as it would be hard to keep such a matter away from the press.

Or, Oberstein has not been handed over because his handover was connected to another matter, but that would not explain Mycroft's anxiety for us to complete our investigation on 28 December – the day before the Jamieson Raid started.

Or, some other matter has intervened to which we are not privy, but which has prevented the handover.

WATSON: And what, if anything, do you think you should do?

HOLMES: I am not sure that I have any further role to play. I have received no further commission from any party. And Oberstein's fate is not my concern.

WATSON: But surely, something unaccountable happening in one of our gaols is something that should concern you, as a good citizen?

At the time of *The Final Problem*, you said that in over a thousand cases, you were unaware that you had ever used your powers upon the wrong side. Does Oberstein's status as a prisoner, murderer, and spy mean you are indifferent to his fate in British custody?

Pause

What do you think Cadogan West would have done in the face of a dilemma such as yours?

HOLMES: Watson, you are right. I have no choice but to investigate this matter. Let justice be done though the heavens fall.

An idea of how to prosecute the investigation is upon me.

Be you ready to come to a summons to Mycroft's ministry at a moment's notice.

Scene X

WATSON: *(to audience):* In the next few weeks I saw my friend hardly at all. But I kept myself ready for a summons and so it was that I was called to meet Holmes at Mycroft's office in his ministry.

MYCROFT: What brings you and Dr Watson here?

HOLMES: I think you realise, Mycroft, that I could hardly let the matter of Oberstein rest. I have conducted my own investigation into why he was not released into German custody after I had discovered his cache of secret documents, and I will lay out my findings to you although I fear they will hardly come as news to you.

MYCROFT: (*stiffly*) Pray continue.

HOLMES: I struck up acquaintance with some warders of Wandsworth Prison by spending time at a local tavern and telling them that I was about to start working in the prison. Once I had had a suitable replica uniform made, it was easy to get into the prison. There I found next to the execution chamber a torture chamber, and an examination of the grounds of the prison revealed a chapel with a freshly dug grave outside the hallowed ground.

MYCROFT: And what is your point, Sherlock?

HOLMES: I believe Oberstein committed suicide on the day we went down to Stonehenge, which explains why you have a recent burial in unconsecrated land. And I believe he was tortured, as a non-German speaker such as Tyler would not have been able to understand any comments that Oberstein made in his sleep. And I fear that a diplomatic price will have to be paid for what has happened.

Long silence

MYCROFT: (*smoothly*) The enhanced interrogation cells at Wandsworth are only used in the most exceptional cases when the British public needs to be protected. They do not constitute physical torture – indeed simulated drowning leaves no mark on the body at all.

HOLMES: What you despatched us to look for was only of interest to the Americans, so you have clearly used it as a bargaining chip with them. You can therefore hardly be said to be defending the interests of the British public.

MYCROFT: As I indicated to you, Sherlock, you are a master of the minutiae of investigations. From an early age, by contrast, you have displayed no grasp at all of the great matters that are afoot in this world. The British have dominated the world in this nineteenth century, but the twentieth century will be an American one. We may provide some of the finesse to the political path that they follow – if I may use a classical allusion, we will be to them advisers as the Greeks were to the Romans in the Roman Empire – but the main direction will be theirs.

HOLMES: So, what did finding Oberstein's cache deliver to you?

MYCROFT: The passing of Oberstein's documents to the Americans has persuaded them to give a solemn undertaking that they will intervene militarily on our side in the event of a major European military conflict. That was a prize worth securing.

HOLMES: And you think it is worth torturing somebody to achieve these ends?

MYCROFT: You yourself thought that Oberstein should end his days on the gallows and, indeed, it is somewhat ironic he should have chosen to hang himself in his cell after Tyler had extracted the information that he did. When you expressed this view, I hardly knew that events would take the course that they have, but the consequence has been the same as what you sought. What has happened was perhaps merely a failure to prevent what might have happened anyway.

Long silence

The banning of advanced interrogation techniques – indeed human rights legislation in general – normally protects the interests of the guilty and not those of the innocent. I share your view that it goes against the grain to apply such techniques to find out about documents which are to be passed to the Americans. But I suspect you might take a different view had the documents endangered British interests.

HOLMES: I think you will find, Mycroft, that my interrogation and investigation techniques have proved equal to bringing to justice the greatest criminals in Europe – aye, even Moriarty, the Napoleon of crime. I am sure that given the time which your grubby deal denied me, I could have tracked down Oberstein's documents without the clues which you extracted in this grotesque manner.

MYCROFT: I think you will find, Sherlock, that the end justifies the means.

HOLMES: But the prize you say you have secured is based on a contingency and is not enforceable. You cannot be sure that there will be a conflict in Europe and, even if there is one, you cannot force the Americans to honour the agreement to come to our aid if the political circumstances have changed in the meantime.

MYCROFT: (*loftily*) The Americans always do the right thing eventually, although they do, I concede, tend to explore every other option first. They are rather like a younger brother to this country, dear Sherlock. They are strong in technical knowledge and in physical power, but deficient in decision-making skills and in political acumen.

HOLMES: And what about the Germans? You have reneged on your squalid agreement with them.

MYCROFT: There too, I can report that a successful outcome has been reached. The Germans expressed no surprise at our *modus operandi*. A spy unmasked, such as Oberstein, would not have been of much use to them anyway. We have agreed with them that the Kaiser will write a telegram to the Boer president, Paul Kruger, congratulating him on the successful quashing of the raid. And it will mention the lack of support given to the raid by the Germans in South West Africa. The Germans think that this will demonstrate their political maturity to the global public.

HOLMES: And how does that help this country?

MYCROFT: I think it will inflame anti-German feeling here, thereby deflecting British attention from the failure of the

Jameson raid and from Oberstein's fate. Thus, all will be well.

And I would give you, Sherlock, and you too, Dr Watson, a piece of advice: Any public reference by either of you to actions you have taken with regard to Oberstein or to the political disclosures I have made to you, will result in consequences that will be blindingly swift, wholly disproportionate, and highly unpleasant.

HOLMES: Are you threatening me?

MYCROFT: You said in the submarine adventure recently concluded that you felt that all the queen's horses and all the queen's men would not avail us. I can assure you that I do indeed have all the queen's horses and all the queen's men at my back. I will not hesitate to have them ride you down should I see fit. You will have no chance. No chance at all. Do you have any other work on at the moment?

Pause.

WATSON: You **are** working on your monograph on medieval music, Holmes..

MYCROFT: Then I would suggest, dear brother, that you focus your energies on that.

A PERILOUS ENGAGEMENT

Dramatis Personae

Sherlock Holmes

Dr John Watson

Ignatius Foley MP

Jean Leckie (F)

Her chaperone

Mycroft Holmes

Buttons

Notes

Foley and Mycroft Holmes can be played by the same actor.

If women play the roles of Holmes, Watson, or Foley, they should be dressed as men.

Mycroft can be played by a woman acting as a woman although this would require some minor textual changes. The chaperone and the buttons can be played by the same person. If a woman is used for the chaperone, she needs to be referred to as Aunt Ethel rather than Uncle Bertram in the first scene.

The same set can be used throughout.

This consists of two chairs facing each other and one in between behind. A large cupboard is in the corner, but it only used in the final scene. There is a fourth chair off to one side for the chaperone in Scenes I and III.

Running time: 24 minutes

Prelude

Stage dark. Sound of a violent scuffle off stage coming to a decisive conclusion.

Lights come on.

Scene I

Jean Leckie, Ignatius Foley, and a chaperone in a sitting room.

LECKIE: And when shall I see you again, dear Ignatius.

FOLEY: I must consult my diary, dearest Jean. I will need to see when my duties as Member of Parliament for Perth permit my return to London.

Reaches into his pocket and, as he pulls his diary out, his pocket disgorges a swirl of small papers.

Foley alarmed

Stand back! Stand back! I must retrieve these papers myself.

Starts to do so.

Leckie and the chaperone rise to help him.

FOLEY: Stand back, I tell you! Stand back!

Gathers up papers

Leckie: (*stiffly*) Uncle Bertram, kindly escort Mr Foley to the door.

Foley exits huffily with chaperone

Leckie sees a paper Foley has missed. Picks it up and looks at it.

LECKIE: How very odd!

Exit Leckie

Stage goes dark. Holmes and Watson take the seats previously occupied by Foley and Leckie.

Scene II

The sitting room at Baker Street.

Enter Buttons.

BUTTONS: Mr Holmes and Dr Watson! Miss Jean Leckie to see you.

Enter Leckie: Exit Buttons.

HOLMES: Pray tell us something about yourself, Madame.

LECKIE: My name you know. I live in Kensington and am of gentle stock. I am unmarried, but I am the fiancée of the Perth MP, Ignatius Foley.

HOLMES: Mr Foley's name is of course known to me, but I understood he was married. Perhaps you would explain your association.

LECKIE: Mr Foley splits his time between his parliamentary duties in London and his Perth constituency where his wife lives. He is a man of means as he had a legal practise before going into politics. His wife is consumptive, and her death is a matter of time. Ignatius and I will marry once his wife is no more.

Pause

Perhaps you find the relationship I have described a troubling one, but I can assure you that relations between Ignatius and me are of conventual purity and will remain so until his marriage reaches its natural end. I am always chaperoned when I am in his company – as was the case yesterday morning when the matter I am about to discuss occurred.

HOLMES: Pray continue.

LECKIE: When Ignatius got his diary out to plan our next meeting, a heap of papers came out of his pocket. He was extremely abrupt and insisted on picking them up himself before leaving in a huff.

When he had gone, I noted that he had failed to retrieve one document.

HOLMES: And what was the document?

LECKIE: It was a rental invoice for a property in London.

HOLMES: What is so unusual about that? I imagine your fiancé must rent a flat for when he is in London on parliamentary duty.

LECKIE: It was not made out to him.

It was addressed to a Mr James Turnavine for the rental of a flat at Denbigh Row in Fitzrovia. Turnavine is the Conservative member for Whitstable whereas Mr Foley is of the governing Liberal party and has a London flat in the Albany. Therefore, the bill was from another member of parliament from a different party, from a different part of the country, and with a residence in a different part of London.

HOLMES: You said your fiancé is a man of means. Could he have bought a property that he has rented out to another Member of Parliament?

LECKIE: That was, Mr Holmes, of course, the first explanation that came to mind, but the invoice is from Fitzrovia Estates, and my research yesterday afternoon showed this is a company belonging to the Duke of Grafton.

HOLMES: You seem to have a remarkable talent for investigative research. What are your next steps to be?

LECKIE: Well, I really came here to hear a theory from you rather than to propose a course of action myself.

HOLMES: Then, dear Madame, I would suggest you return home and I will consider the matter. Please come back immediately if more material comes to light.

Exit Leckie

Loud bang from the street door. Sound of footsteps coming up the stairs. Enter Buttons and Mycroft Holmes.

BUTTONS: Mr Holmes and Dr Watson! Mr Mycroft Holmes to see you.

Exit Buttons

MYCROFT: Sherlock, dear brother, as the chief advisor to the Prime Minister, I need you to go to the continent immediately. I will travel with you to Victoria Station to meet a man from the Bulgarian secret police. There is not a moment to lose. You will need to travel to Sofia, and there is an express to Dover at noon. You will be in the Bulgarian capital by tomorrow evening.

(to Watson) I fear, Doctor Watson, that the Bulgarian authorities were most insistent that only my brother should come and help them.

HOLMES: Very well, good brother. I know your importance in British government circles and will do what I can to serve my country.

MYCROFT: As will I, dear brother, as will I.

Exeunt Sherlock Holmes and Mycroft Holmes

Watson sits looking at the bill when there is a tap on the door.

WATSON: Come

Enter Leckie

LECKIE: Is Mr Holmes not here?

WATSON: He has been called away on urgent business. I cannot tell you when he will return.

LECKIE: I feared that might be so. Would you have time to look at my petition before you go out – I see you have only one more cigarette in your case, so your need to go to the tobacconist is urgent.

Watson glances into his cigarette case

WATSON: I am happy to do so, Madame, but I would advise you that my previous efforts at detective work have had mixed results.

Pause

LECKIE *(voice full of emotion):* Dr Watson, I need to talk to someone I can trust.

She passes a scrap of paper to Dr Watson

I returned home and sat in the lounge. It felt cold, and I decided to add some coals to the fire. In the scuttle I found this bill from an establishment called the Bar of Gold in Upper Swandham Lane in London's docklands. The only entry on it is, 'Two pipes at four shillings.'

WATSON: (*gravely*) Madame, I could not put any sort of construction on the rental bill you said came from your fiancé but addressed to another MP. This document, by contrast, is from a notorious opium den known to me because of a case I undertook with Mr Holmes. I fear you will find its explanation only discreditable.

LECKIE: You say so, Dr Watson, and that was my immediate reaction too, yet your conclusion leaves so much unclarified.

If the Bar of Gold is a dubious establishment, why would it issue a receipt, and why would anyone wish to keep it? And look at the date on the bill. It is from 25th January of last year, that is to say, 1906.

Why would my fiancé have it in his pocket a year after it was issued?

And I made a further discovery.

I keep a careful record both of my movements of those of my betrothed so that we can see each other as often as possible while allowing hm to attend to his duties to his constituents and to his wife. My records showed that on the evening of 24th January last year, my chaperone and I accompanied Ignatius to Euston Station whence he boarded the night train to Perth.

WATSON: Could he have alighted at an intermediate stop and returned to London?

LECKIE: Dear Dr Watson, 25th January is, of course, Burns Night. My local library gets copies of both national and local newspapers. After this discovery I repaired there and consulted The Perth Weekly Informer of January last year. It says 'The Perth Society of Whisky Producers held its annual Burns Night supper yesterday evening. After the piping in of the haggis, the members were addressed by Perth's member of Parliament, Mr Ignatius Foley.'

My betrothed was four hundred or more miles from the Bar of Gold on 25 January of last year.

WATSON: *(awestruck)* I fear, Madame, I am unable to advise you on this matter although I would echo Mr Holmes's remarks about your investigative skills.

Pause

LECKIE: Good Dr Watson, my discussions with you have hardened my resolve. I will confront my betrothed, Mr Foley, with my findings when he is back in London next week. Could you act as my chaperone? I would rather you acted as my witness than anyone from my family.

WATSON: I think you are right to clarify matters on what strikes me as a most perilous engagement, dear lady. I shall be happy to help you. Who will you say that I am?

LECKIE: I have an Uncle Horace whom Ignatius has heard of but has never met. I will introduce you as him.

WATSON: Madame, you have an answer for everything.

Stage goes dark

Scene III

At the Leckie house. Leckie, Foley, Watson as chaperone.

FOLEY: (*perkily*) And Miss Jean, how would you like at, some point in the future, to be Lady Foley? For I am to be made attorney general quite soon. The post carries with it not only a princely salary but a knighthood.

LECKIE: Why this sudden political advancement? How can a man with a constituency in a distant part of the country, a sick wife, and a pining fiancée assume high office?

FOLEY: Events, dear Jean, events. The Prime Minister was most insistent I should take the post, and I would be most reluctant to disoblige him.

LECKIE: Ignatius, I have a matter of great concern which I would like to raise with you. What were a bill from an opium den, and a rental invoice made out to another man doing in your pocket?

You failed to pick them up when your pocket disgorged a pile of documents that you were most anxious I should not help you pick up.

I can think of no reason that is not discreditable to someone for the bill from the opium den and I have no explanation at all for the rental bill.

FOLEY: I can give you my word that I have never been to any opium den.

LECKIE: You may be surprised to know I regard that as possible as I was able to establish that you were not in London on the day the bill was raised. But that does not explain its presence in your pocket.

And why was a rental bill of another MP in your pocket?

FOLEY: Which one?

LECKIE: (*suddenly angry*) That is of no matter. I can think of no satisfactory explanation for either document being on your person.

FOLEY: (*suavely*) In politics, dear lady, one's enemies are in one's own party as it is with them I am in competition for ministerial preference. I am accordingly in regular though not frequent discussion with members of other parties.

LECKIE: That hardly explains why you would have a document personal to another member of parliament. Does this flirtation with a member of another political party have anything to do with your political advancement?

FOLEY: How could dealings with a member of another party enable me to win the favour of the prime minister?

LECKIE: (*suddenly passionate*) It is **I** who must ask the questions. It is **I** who is sacrificing her youth so that we can marry when you are free. You have already had a life with another. I am hoping to have one with you and have foresworn all others to do so.

What, I repeat, have these documents to do with your sudden political advancement?

FOLEY: I would refer you to my previous responses to your questions.

LECKIE: I will have to consider our position.

I had hoped you would have an answer that put my concerns to rest but you have not. Our relations are of much more moment than a mere flirtation between a man old enough to know better and a girl who, alas, does not.

I will write if I wish to see you again.

Uncle Horace, please escort Mr Foley to the door.

Exeunt Leckie, Foley, and Watson

Stage goes dark. Holmes and Watson take the seats previously occupied by Foley and Leckie.

Scene IV

The sitting room at Baker Street.

WATSON: It is good to have you back from Bulgaria, Holmes. Miss Leckie's case has become only more mysterious over the last two weeks. She found a second bill left behind by her affianced - this time from that notorious opium den, the Bar of Gold. And yet she had clear evidence that Mr Foley was not there on the night the bill was made out.

HOLMES: You missed nothing in not joining me in Bulgaria. The case Mycroft sent me on was remarkably trivial. By contrast, this Leckie matter strikes me as important.

WATSON: Really? I appreciate the fair Miss Leckie has a personal dilemma, but I hardly think a private matter like hers compares to a matter of state like the one in Sofia.

HOLMES: Good Watson, I must commend your gallantry in acting as Miss Leckie's chaperone and, in addition, praise her investigative skills. But you have both missed the solution to a case that is trivial in substance, grave in the way it would be perceived by the public, and of great consequence to her personally.

WATSON: Perhaps you could explain.

HOLMES: I will start with the somewhat facile resolution of the case although I will have to conduct one interview to confirm my solution.

WATSON: So, what were these documents?

HOLMES: Neither of the documents Leckie retrieved were his. And he had no idea of precisely what documents he was carrying as he attached great importance to their recovery but failed to realise afterwards that he had not retrieved them all. The inference to be drawn from that is obvious.

Long pause

Where, Watson, might you find administrative documents in large numbers belonging to several or many different people?

WATSON: I would say at the post office, but I hardly think that Mr Foley would be taking documents from a post office.

HOLMES: Not in a post office, dear Watson, but in an **accounts** office. Mr Foley has broken into an accounts office and grabbed as many accounting documents as he could lay his hands upon.

WATSON: Can you prove which accounts office?

HOLMES: I will need to conduct one interview with...

Door opens

BUTTONS: Mr Mycroft Holmes to see you, Mr Holmes.

Enter Mycroft

MYCROFT: It is good to see you back from Bulgaria, dear brother. I have another commission for you which will also require your absence from London.

HOLMES: Good day to you, brother Mycroft. I too have a matter I would raise with you.

MYCROFT: Be brief, good brother. It is crucial that you undertake this second overseas mission immediately, and most undesirable that I be away from Westminster for any length of time. It gives the Prime Minister and his acolytes the impression that they can run the country without me.

HOLMES: Very well. Why then, may I ask, as a good citizen of this country, have you not called the police in to investigate the recent burglary of the accounts office of the Houses of Parliament or the Serjeant-at-Arms' Office, as it is normally called?

MYCROFT: (*startled*) How do you know about that? I have taken the most extreme measures to make sure that that does not get into the press just yet. (*shiftily*) I would even go so far as to say that your fruitless mission to Bulgaria was not unconnected with it.

Pause

Parliament has been rocked with rumours that members have been submitting inappropriate expense claims. If it got out, there would be general outrage and the role of our parliamentary representatives, aye even of Parliament itself, would be called into question.

Just over two weeks ago, an intruder was apprehended by one of our night security staff. The trespasser was just leaving the office of the Serjeant-at-Arms where the expense records of members of Parliament are kept. After a struggle, the intruder fled but a briefcase was prised from his grasp. When the matter was reported to me, I had the intruder brought before me, and made sure I was the only person present when I forced the case open.

Mycroft takes a large pinch of snuff.

I found it contained all the expense claims for the last two years from members of Parliament whose surnames ran from N to T.

HOLMES: What were the claims for?

MYCROFT: For some of the most outlandish things. Alongside claims for overnight accommodation and travel, one member had claimed to have a swimming pool built, another had claimed to have turrets put on his house, and a third had claimed on an invoice from an establishment, the nature of which I could not possibly disclose.

HOLMES: And to whom did you report the burglary if not the police?

MYCROFT: Naturally I reported the matter to the Prime Minister.

HOLMES: And how did the Prime Minister react?

MYCROFT: The burglary had, of course, been carried out on the Prime Minister's instructions. He was horrified that its objectives had been thwarted. Like me, he felt that it was best that the matter obtained the smallest possible coverage. There will be a cabinet reshuffle shortly. The Prime Minister has assured me the intruder will be appointed to a ministerial post in which he will be able to ensure nothing will be done to investigate the break-in.

HOLMES: And what else did you do?

MYCROFT: I went down to the office of the Serjeant-at-Arms and made sure the filing cabinets with members' expense claims were emptied and their contents burned.

HOLMES: What will you do next?

MYCROFT: In a few days' time, I shall ensure that a discrete mention is made of the burglary in some minor organ of the press.

HOLMES: Why will you do that?

MYCROFT: Well, obviously, if the main body of the press gets hold of the much bigger story of fraudulent expense claims by members of Parliament, I can then tell them that all documentary evidence of the claims has been destroyed.

I will point out the previously published account of the burglary. Fleet Street's embarrassment at having failed to notice this story, will stop them pursuing the matter of the expenses of members of Parliament any further.

Thus, all will be well.

HOLMES: And did you get all the incriminating evidence of inappropriate claims?

MYCROFT: Investigative details, dear brother, are more an area for your expertise than for mine. It is possible that the intruder had further documents on his person but as his objective was to destroy evidence of wrongdoing, he will doubtless have taken steps to give effect to that in any case.

HOLMES: And I assume you have rewarded the member of security staff who apprehended the intruder. To take on and apprehend an intruder single-handed at night would have taken significant courage.

MYCROFT: On the contrary, good brother, a separate investigation into the timekeeping of our security staff has revealed lapses of accuracy by both the apprehender of the intruder and some of his colleagues. They have all been advised that no action will be taken now. But the matter can be re-opened at any time.

Pause

And now for the commission at hand. This will take you to some of our most far-flung colonies – probably for several months. And I can assure you that there may be a knighthood at the end of it.

And, in the circumstances, Dr Watson may wish to accompany you, and there may be an honour in this for him as well.

HOLMES: I fear that I cannot allow myself to be manoeuvred out of the country to allow you to manoeuvre your way out of a political embarrassment.

Pause

MYCROFT: (*threatening suavely*) In that case, dear brother, I would advise you and Dr Watson to keep this matter to yourselves. Any public reference to it will have, shall we say, unfortunate consequences for you and anyone else you communicate to. I wish you a good morning.

Exit Mycroft

HOLMES: You see Watson, only a burglary in the office of the Serjeant-at-Arms explanation fitted the facts.

Only an accounts office would hold personal invoices from a number of different people, and only one located in the Houses of Parliament would hold invoices from politicians. And only a burglary would explain how Mr Foley could have been in possession of such personal documents which clearly did not relate to him, and the only value of the documents was that the bearer of them could claim expenses on them.

And only an attempt to cover up a scandal would explain why no news of the break-in had leaked out.

WATSON: And why would an establishment such as the Bar of Gold issue a receipt to someone who patronised it?

HOLMES: Because the Member of Parliament who frequented it asked for one. Being a Member of Parliament is very far from being a full-time occupation. So, our representatives seek diversions to combat their ennui. But they can only be recompensed if they have a document to claim against.

WATSON: And what are you going to tell Miss Leckie?

Long silence

LECKIE (*from a hiding place*): Yes, what will you tell me?

Leckie emerges quite undiscommoded by her period of concealment.

LECKIE: I had already worked out that my fiancé's action had serious political consequences, Mr Holmes and I know your brother's role in government. When I saw a man who looked like you mounting the stairs as I left here two weeks ago, that confirmed it.

I banged the street door closed but hid myself in the hallway till the buttons had gone back to his duties. I then crept back up the stairs, listened outside your door to your brother's petition, and realised that he was trying to get you out of the country.

I watched every boat train at Victoria and, when I saw you descend from the boat train today, sprang into a hansom, and beat you back to Baker Street.

On my arrival here, I was asked to wait downstairs, as you were not in, and Dr Watson had not risen from his slumbers. When breakfast was laid out for Dr Watson, it was an obvious step to conceal myself here.

HOLMES: You are a remarkable woman, but you are in great danger. Although he did not divulge the intruder's identity to us, Mycroft will be able to identify who the intruder's antecedents are, and he is almost bound to want to investigate how I got to know about this matter. You heard what threats he issued against me. What do you think he might do to you?

LECKIE: Are you suggesting that I need some form of protection? I am sure I am capable of looking after myself.

HOLMES: I have no doubt that you are more than equal to most threats, but here all the forces of the state will be arrayed against you. I do indeed believe you will need someone of courage and dedication to protect you.

WATSON: (hesitantly) I should myself be most happy to offer my services.

LECKIE: (*warmly*) Good Dr Watson. I greatly admire your behaviour towards me. I can think of no one else whom I would rather have to protect me from peril.

Watson and Leckie embrace

Pause

HOLMES: Madame, your choice is an excellent one. I can think of no one better suited to protect you than my good friend, Dr Watson.

Very well, then what Sherlock Holmes has brought together, let no man put asunder.

FINIS

MR DEVINE'S ORIGINAL PROBLEM

Dramatis personae

Sherlock Holmes

Dr John Watson

Mr Devine

Running time: 10 minutes

Notes

All parts can be played by men or by women

Only Scene

HOLMES: I note, good Watson, that our client, Mr Devine, is a creative spirit whose strong hands are skilled at the plane and the lathe. His use of these old tools leads me to surmise that he is rather older than his outward appearance would suggest. And the alluvial mud I see adhering to the welt of his boot shows me that he comes from the Middle East as nowhere else is there a place where there are four distinct riverheads, one of which flows through gold bearing rock.

MR DEVINE: What you say, Mr Holmes, has the accuracy for which you are famed. My boots bear traces of mud from four rivers that have their headwaters in the Middle East. The Pishon is known for its gold. Aromatic resin and onyx are also there. The other rivers are the Gihon, the Tigris, and the Euphrates.

And even if your eyes tell each of you that I am the same age as each of you, I can confirm that I am indeed a good deal older than people take me for.

It was in the land bounded by the flow of these rivers, years ago beyond measure, and as an outcome of my creative bent, that the events on which I would consult with you occurred.

For it was then that I made a creation in my own image.

WATSON: You mean you painted a self-portrait?

HOLMES: *(caustically)* I hardly think, Watson, that Mr Devine would have come all the way from the Middle East to consult with us on a self-portrait.

I assume, Mr Devine, that your creation was of greater significance than a self-portrait. And that the matter on which you wish to consult with us is consequently also of greater significance.

MR DEVINE: That is so. I would not wish to go into any more detail on the creative process itself but the results of it were a man and a woman for whom I found quarters in a well-watered garden.

All would have been well, if the two had not made a self-discovery.

WATSON: *(to audience)*: At this point our client gave us an account of the nature of the self-discovery, which I could not possibly disclose in a work designed for publication in this last decade of the nineteenth century. In any case, precise details of it have no bearing on the petition that followed.

MR DEVINE: I am here, to ask you, Mr Holmes what response I should make to the two. Their self-discovery is an act of disobedience which requires chastisement. I therefore have banished them from the place they lived and will not allow them back.

WATSON: Does that not seem rather final?

MR DEVINE: In my realm, my powers are supreme and my judgments binding, But I am able to adjust whatever I choose to adjust at any time after the event, and in any way that I choose.

HOLMES: So, if I may summarise your petition, it is that you would wish me to suggest a suitable punishment for these creations of yours whom you regard as malefactors?

MR DEVINE: That is so. Perhaps in the narratives of your friend here there are cases which parallel my petition?

HOLMES: There was, of course, the case of the Beryl Coronet. There, Mary Holder, the much-loved niece and adoptive daughter of my client, the wealthy banker, Mr Alexander Holder, stole a valuable piece of jewellery, which was in his possession, but which was not his. She passed it to the ruined gambler, Sir George Burnwell. She allowed my client's son, Arthur, to take the blame for the jewellery's theft and then eloped with Sir George. I commented at the time that this display of free will might of itself bring a suitable punishment down on her.

MR DEVINE: What relevance has that to my petition?

HOLMES: If free will can itself be a punishment, then that will spare you the need to devise a punishment yourself.

MR DEVINE: You make yourself very plain.

WATSON: But whatever the punishment you deem fitting, Holmes, and however it is exacted, you have failed to specify any duration for it. Surely, no trespass can merit a punishment without end.

Pause

MR DEVINE: What happened to your client's son, who was falsely accused of stealing the coronet?

WATSON: He subsequently tracked down his cousin, Mary, although she had asked that no attempt be made to do so. He was in love with her, but she would not have him. Nevertheless, this love for her caused him to intercede with his father, and your client was eventually prevailed upon to allow her back into his house, where she was able to lead a life of some ease.

MR DEVINE: As well as my two creations, I also have a natural son. Maybe, at some point, I will prevail upon him to intercede on behalf of the two expellees from the garden of whom I spoke, just as love drove Arthur Holder to intercede for his cousin with his father.

Exit Mr Devine

HOLMES: It was love that motivated Arthur Holder to intercede for his cousin, Mary, even though she had allowed him to take the blame for something for which she was responsible, and even though she did not return his love.

Now, I think, I shall dedicate my attention to music.

I have never loved a specific person, good Watson. Yet love in the wider sense seems to be what brings out the best of all of us in terms of forgiveness, generosity, and advocacy of others.

Sound of the opening of The Lark Ascending by Ralph Vaughan Williams

It protects, trusts, hopes, and perseveres.

FINIS

APPENDIX

OPENING OF THE CAMBERWELL TYRANT (if performed as a stand-alone play)

Scene I

Sitting-room at Baker Street

Holmes, Watson, James Windibank

HOLMES: The man married a woman older than himself for her money and enjoyed the use of daughter's money as long as she lived with them. It was evident that with her fair personal advantages, and her little income, she would be gone from the family home taking her personal income with her.

So what does her stepfather do?

He covers those keen eyes with tinted glasses, masks the face with a moustache and a pair of bushy whiskers, sinks that clear voice into an insinuating whisper, and doubly secure on account of the girl's short sight, appears as Mr Hosmer Angel.

WINDIBANK: It was only a joke at first. We never thought that she would have been so carried away.

HOLMES: Very likely not. However that may be, the young lady was very decidedly carried away, the suspicion of treachery never for an instant entered her mind.

But the deception could not be kept up forever.

And nothing could be better calculated to stop her looking at another than an engagement and an unexplained abandonment at the church door re-enforced by vows of fidelity exacted upon a Testament. James Windibank wished Miss Sutherland to be so bound to Hosmer Angel, and so uncertain as to his fate, that for ten years to come, at any rate, she would not listen to another man.

WINDIBANK: *Rising from his chair*

It may be so, or it may not, Mr Holmes. But if you are so very sharp you ought to be sharp enough to know that it is you who are breaking the law now, and not me. I have done nothing actionable from the first, but as long as you keep that door locked, you lay yourself open to an action for assault and illegal constraint.

HOLMES: The law cannot, as you say, touch you. Yet there never was a man who deserved punishment more. If the young lady has a brother or a friend, he ought to lay a whip across your shoulders. By Jove, it is not part of my duties to my client, but here's a hunting crop handy, and I think I shall just treat myself to—"

Holmes takes two swift steps to the whip

Windibank flees

HOLMES: There's a cold-blooded scoundrel. He will rise from crime to crime until he does something very bad, and ends on a gallows.

WATSON: So what will you do now?

The Redacted Sherlock Holmes – The Stories

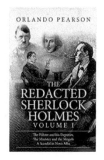 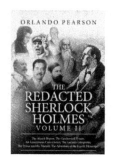 

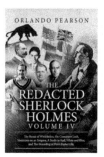  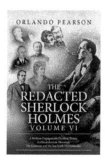

The redacted Sherlock Holmes stories Volumes 1-6

Also available from MX Publishing

MX Publishing is the largest Sherlock Holmes publisher in the world with over 500 books and more than two hundred authors.

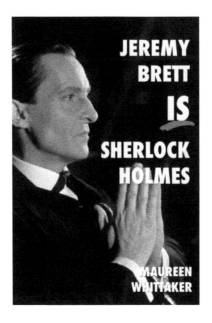

You can find out all about MX and our social enterprise at mxpublishing.com, on Twitter and Instagram @mxpublishing and on facebook.com/mxpublishing

Milton Keynes UK
Ingram Content Group UK Ltd.
UKHW051451010724
444990UK00043B/1224